RAGE

Sergio Bizzio

Translated by Amanda Hopkinson

BITTER LEMON PRESS
LONDON

BITTER LEMON PRESS

First published in the United Kingdom in 2009 by
Bitter Lemon Press, 37 Arundel Gardens, London W11 2LW

www.bitterlemonpress.com

First published in Spanish as *Rabia* by
El Cobre Ediciones, S.L., Barcelona, 2004

Bitter Lemon Press gratefully acknowledges the financial
assistance of the Arts Council of England

A CIP record for this book is available from the British
Library ISBN 978–1–904738–40-4

Typeset by Alma Books Limited
Printed and bound by Cox & Wyman Ltd. Reading, Berkshire

Rage

"'You really give it a lot of importance if you let it control your life like this,' I told him, and he replied: 'Would you like to know whether or not I want to hear what you're saying?'"

"Did he say that?"

"No. He let me understand that was what he meant."

Doctor Wayne W. Dyer & Lua Senku, *Dialogues*

1

"When you were born I was just coming..."

"I don't believe you," said Rosa, laughing, "you can't possibly remember something like that..."

There were fifteen years between them. Rosa was twenty-five and José María forty years old. He was so in love with her, he thought himself capable of anything, even down to remembering what he was doing at the time of her birth: was he actually screwing? At that point in time, he was going out with a very tall, very thin girl, who straightened up every time he put his hand on her waist, making herself appear even taller and bonier than she was already. The girl was a good head taller than him, wore tight lycra and ironed her hair, and she had a stammer. In spite of it all, they had sex. José María had been in a relationship with the girl all year: there was one chance in twenty-eight that they were actually making love on the day that Rosa was born (February). He thought about it in *days* not in *seconds*; he was unable to ignore that, according to Dr Dyer, "if an orgasm lasted three minutes, nobody would believe in God"; in addition, if he got his memory to think in such tiny units of time, it would have amounted to putting his own existence in doubt. In any case, it was a joke, a game. And Rosa was enchanted by the very idea. She embraced him.

He let her cover his face with kisses. When Rosa's ear came close to his mouth, he took the opportunity to ask her:

"Can I take you from behind?"

Rosa froze.

"Oh…" she replied.

"What's the matter?"

"I was scared you were going to get around to asking me that one of these days…"

"Don't you want me to?"

"It's just that…"

Rosa often left her sentences unfinished. She was highly excited, but starting and stopping while leaving her sentences unfinished was her usual form of speech; it had nothing to do with her state of excitement. She thought at the speed of light, and her thoughts clashed and intercepted one another.

"You'll like it…"

"I'm not sure…"

"I can assure you."

José María regarded her a moment in silence and, since Rosa said nothing, he lowered himself from on top of her, lay down at her side and put his hand on her waist to turn her over. But Rosa arched her back and moved away rapidly, as if José María's hand had given her an electric shock.

"What's up?"

She shook her head.

"Come on, Rosa, I mean what I'm saying…"

Rosa propped herself on one elbow across the bed, looked at him and asked:

"Do you love me?"

"You know very well I do…"

"So why do you want to make me…?"

"My love, how on earth does that have anything to do with it? We've been going out together for two months… Do you really love me?"

"I adore you."

"Well, I adore you too!"

"I knew that one day you'd come to me with…"

"You knew it because you too wanted it. *That's why* you knew it."

"The problem is, it's that I've never…"

"And I've never done it either!"

"Really?"

"Why on earth would I lie to you?"

"You've never made love like that… with anyone?"

José María bunched his fingers and kissed them, swearing on the form of the cross. The two of them were totally naked in a little hotel room down on the Bajo, where they went on Saturdays. The only thing they were wearing was their watches. Only last week José María had bought two fake Rolexes and given one to Rosa.

José María managed to read the time on Rosa's Rolex: it was twenty to twelve. Soon it would be noon. The time they would have to vacate the room.

"You weren't lying to me?"

"What do you want, that I swear it you again? I'll swear from here to China if you want. I swear solemnly before God."

"I believe you. How idiotic, if I tell you 'I believe you', you'll think that I'm giving in…"

"Darling, let's not talk about it any more. We just have twenty minutes left…"

"And in twenty minutes you want to do… Twenty minutes is no time at all for such a thing!"

"Rosa, I love you."

"Yes, I know you do…"

"What does time matter if we're in love?"

"It's just that for me it's all very…"

"Just try it, whatever. Let me try it. Let's try it to-gether."

"And if it hurts me?"

"What do you mean, hurts you? If it hurts you, I'll stop."

"Will you love me just the same afterwards?"

José María beamed at her.

"Come here, give me a kiss…" he told her.

Rosa kissed him, but only after a pause: she knew that the kiss meant "yes".

Beneath her reluctance, she was dying for it. She would have given him everything and anything. If he'd had two cocks, he could have given it to her with both. She loved him. Her fear wasn't that it would hurt, or even that he would lose his respect for her. The truth was that she was not afraid of anything. Her desire overwhelmed her, in the exact same way as her thoughts ran ahead of her words; that was all. No, really nothing more: she simply hadn't foreseen the time when José María would ask to take her from behind.

They had got to know one another in the queue at the Disco supermarket. José María was a construction worker; Rosa was a maid in the villa belonging to the Blinder family. He had left the site where he'd been working (as yet still a skeleton two blocks away from the mansion) to buy meat and bread for their midday fry-up and had ended up in the line, right behind Rosa, who had been going for her weekly shop: her trolley was overflowing. José María calculated that the young woman had enough purchases to guarantee a good half-hour at the till. He slid a glance at the tills on either side, but the queues were even longer, and an ill-tempered tutting escaped from under his breath. Rosa heard him: she looked at the red plastic basket José María was holding in one hand (containing one packet with bread in it and another with cuts of meat) and said:

"Would you like to go through first?"

José María was caught off-guard by her offer. He raised his eyebrows and made a strange movement with his head, both shaking it and nodding at the same time.

"No, I'm fine where I am, no problem…"

He wasn't used to any kind of friendliness. That was why, when Rosa began to take her purchases out of the trolley, he interpreted her offer as having been more of a reaction to the impatient teeth-clicking sound he'd made a minute before, when he spotted the huge quantity of goods she had bought and was estimating how long it would take her to get through the till with them.

"I didn't mean…"

Rosa turned and looked at him. She looked at him seriously, silently.

"It's just that I didn't mean…" he repeated.

Sometimes he found it particularly hard to make himself understood.

Rosa resumed leaning over her trolley and continued unloading her shopping.

"Thank you all the same," persisted José María.

"Don't mention it."

The till operator smiled and lowered her gaze to the carton of milk she had in her hand, as she typed in the bar code, thinking that this guy and girl had something going, or else they soon would. She wasn't wrong.

Once Rosa had finished her shopping (she requested the lot be delivered to the tradesman's entrance at the villa) and had come out of the supermarket, she didn't leave immediately. She crossed the street and remained within José María's field of vision, pretending to window-shop. José María emerged a minute later, his bag of purchases dangling from one finger. He crossed the street directly over to where she was.

"Am I bothering you?" he asked.

Rosa had seen his reflection in the window, but feigned surprise, even starting a little. She went so far as to allow an "Ay…" to escape as she raised her hand to her heart.

"You gave me such a fright!"

"I'm sorry."

"It's nothing…"

"Are you from around here?"

"From over there," replied Rosa, pointing at the villa on the corner.

"Some cottage, eh?" observed José María. "I work on the opposite corner, just around there…"

"Ah, yes…"

"Yes. I always come here to do my shopping."

"And what's your line of work?"

"Construction."

"Well, that has to be good…"

"Yes. Plenty going on at the moment."

"What?"

"In construction. Last year there wasn't any work. Now things are picking up. How about you?"

"I'm a maid. It's OK."

José María smiled to himself as if he had suddenly remembered something, and held out his hand.

"I'm José María," he said.

"Rosa," she said, holding out her own.

"Pleased to meet you."

"Me too."

"So, Rosa…"

"Yes…"

"Do you always come here to do your shopping too?"

"It's the only supermarket around here…"

"And this place is so well stocked. It even sells records.

The other day I saw Shakira's latest on sale... Do you like Shakira?"

"Wow. She sure has a voice..."

"What kind of music do you like?"

"Hmmm... Cristian Castro... Iglesias..."

"Father or son?"

"Son, all my life long. The Señora listens to the father when she's alone. But not when other people are around. When there are guests she puts on classical music..." Then she added, smiling, "And they tell her: 'Oh please, turn it off, Rita,' but she just carries on... I've no idea why she plays it if even she doesn't like it!"

"She doesn't like it but she plays it? How weird people are... So it's Enrique Iglesias you prefer. He's called Enrique, isn't he?"

"Yes, Enrique. But I like Cristian Castro better, he really gets to me..."

"And you don't like *cumbia* at all?"

"I used to. Now I've grown a bit tired of it."

"Me too. And I grew up with *cumbia*. My old woman told me that when she was pregnant with me she'd put on the radio and it got to me through the umbilical cord. Think about it. But you're right, in the end you grow tired of it."

"It's not the same for me. I don't like it just because I never liked it. But there are people who like it and will always like it..."

"Yet a minute ago you told me that you used to like it!..."

"No, the truth is that I never really did. What happened was that I didn't want to offend you because it seemed that you..."

"Yes, you're right, *cumbia* touches my soul. Why would I lie to you about that?"

"Incredible, isn't it? We've only just got to know each other and we're already telling lies…"

"Well, they're not really lies," said José María, introducing a sense of proportion. "It's just a topic of conversation, like any other. We adapt what we say out of respect for the other person…"

"It's prudent. And quite right too."

"Perfectly."

"That's the way it has to be. To me prudence seems… Well, when someone tells you the truth just like that…"

"But you look like you're completely sincere…"

"Thank you."

"No, no I mean it seriously! I can look at you and see a sincere person. What did you tell me your name was?"

"Rosa."

"Rosa. That's a pretty name."

"Thank you. Well…"

"Do you have to go?"

The conversation ran on along these lines for a few more minutes, because they felt an attraction, and because neither wanted to end it. They hadn't shifted an inch from the spot on which they stood, seeming rooted to the ground; despite the fact they were shifting from side to side constantly, they were essentially skirting around the same place, leaning forwards from the waist, as if the power of attraction had caused them to lose their sense of balance.

The doorman standing at the entrance to the adjacent building stared at them out of the corner of his eye. He had seen the woman a thousand times previously, always alone, but this was the first time he saw the man, and he didn't approve of the manner in which he observed him address her. Planted at the entrance of the building next door, the doorman was making considerable efforts to overhear their conversation; he caught snatches of it, odd phrases – things like "Who did you vote for?" "No comment, voting is done in secret" – and felt a tide of indignation rising in his throat. It was clear the unknown man was in the act of deliberately seducing the Blinders' maidservant.

The district lacked a code of conduct, yet everyone behaved as if they conformed to one. Even without it, things ran on much as usual. Rather, there was an instinctive code, running deeper than any externally imposed one (it had to do with the quality of one's clothes, with skin and hair colour, with a way of speaking or walking), and which, of course, included domestic staff. In general terms, what happened was that strangers were "*signalled*", principally on sight, leaving them with the sensation of being spied on: it was a highly effective form of insolence, swallowed and put into practice by the entire district, even by household pets. In effect, the doorman would rapidly leave off observing them askance in order to stare openly at them, even taking a step in their direction the better to listen to what they were saying.

He didn't hear overmuch: it was just at the point when José María and Rosa were saying goodbye. The one thing he managed to hear clearly was the promise they made to meet up again. Rosa then set off rapidly in the direction of the villa. José María gazed after her for a few moments, then turned around and set off back to work.

He passed the doorman, whistling and swinging the bag containing the meat for the grill. The doorman, more brazen now that José María was leaving, took a step forwards as if distracted and wishing to examine something on the edge of the pavement, then put himself right in the way of José María. It happened as

rapidly as if he'd planned it: he wanted to force José
María to go around him, so that he could turn on his
heels and follow him with his eyes: a clear insult. What
didn't figure in the doorman's calculations (he was a
fat and flabby fellow with rounded shoulders, somewhat
unobservant despite everything) was that the unknown
man would take deep offence.

"What are you staring at, you idiot?" asked José María,
without halting.

The doorman was struck dumb, and stood there as if
paralysed. By the time he could summon up a reaction,
José María was already at the corner.

"Good God, he's so agile," he thought. "I bet the guy
could leap from one pavement to the next without
landing on the street."

A few hours later that same day, he saw him again. It
was six-thirty in the evening, to be precise. The doorman had now washed and changed his clothes and
was back in the entrance to his building making his
perpetual and enormous effort to appear bored. José
María had completed his day's work: he too had washed
and changed his clothes and was now walking towards
the Blinders' villa.

It was the first time that he had taken this route at
the end of his working day. As a matter of course he
went down the street from his workplace towards the
Bajo, where he caught the minibus in the direction of
his home in Capilla del Señor. Even thinking about the
two hours of journey ahead made him feel tired. He
passed the doorman and nodded.

"Hey you," said the doorman.

José María stopped. Then stared at him. He didn't
look him up and down, but stared him right in the eyes
and asked:

"What's the matter with you?"

"What did I do to you?"

"What d'you mean?"

"This morning you called me an idiot?"

"I apologize. This morning I was chatting here with a young lady, and you were eyeing us up and down and… you know how these things are. Do we know each other?"

"I don't think so."

"That's why I mention it. It's rude to go round staring at people you don't know like that, plus you pushed me off the pavement. That's why I called you an idiot."

"I didn't like the look of you."

"Ah well, what do you want me to do about that?"

"At least you could apologize…"

José María was tired, and hadn't the least desire to get involved in an argument. So he cracked a small smile and carried on walking away. The doorman stood in the middle of the pavement – and, as he watched him depart, considered calling him back a thousand times over, even mentally trying out a number of different tones of voice, but couldn't even manage another "hey you". Frustrated and furious, he went inside his house. He slammed the door so hard that his wife dropped the salt cellar into the saucepan.

"The fucking whore who gave birth to those damn blacks…" he said as he dialled a phone number. "Hello, Israel?" Israel could hear him swearing at the other end of the line. "It's me, Gustavo," continued the doorman. "Are you busy?"

Israel rolled his eyeballs.

"Get to the point, Gustavo," he said. "I'm in the middle of eating…"

"I'll call back later then…"

"No, you tell me what's going on…"

Meanwhile, José María had paused on the corner of the Alvear and Rodríquez Avenues to gaze at the villa. The windows were dark, all except the kitchen windows on the ground floor, and one more on the first floor. The house was imposing: grey in colour, with patches of lichen, and missing plaster here and there, like smoke rings, but you didn't need to be particularly cultured to observe the splendid aura in which it was enveloped. Without looking any further, even the flight of white marble steps dropping down from the front door terminated in the garden with such plasticity it gave the impression of a tiered wedding cake. "How beautiful," he thought. He scratched an armpit and began repeating under his breath "Rosa… Rosita…" – scarcely moving his lips. It was a call… He had never done anything like this before. He had to be falling in love. Yet his heart was beating just the same as ever, with the same rhythm and intensity. Just then one of those sudden gusts of wind arose that sweep up everything one by one: the wind lifted a newspaper page from the ground in order to deposit it a few yards further on, it shook the crown of a treetop, caused a piece of cardboard to vibrate, rise and vanish into the distance. People began to hurry their steps. José María raised his face to the skies: great swathes of dark blue, heavy with stars, but the storm was out there, held within no more than a dozen clouds, all on the point of exploding.

2

The next day not a drop fell and the sky shone like a mirror. José María was made fun of when he arrived at work carrying an umbrella. "It's just that I get up at five in the morning and you lot only got out of bed ten minutes ago," he told the foreman, a strong stocky man with a moustache worthy of Dalí, who took the lead in sorting people out. At such an hour (seven in the morning) no one had the least glimmer of a sense of humour, meaning they tended to indulge in petty remarks, cheap jokes and vulgar gibes. The foreman didn't take kindly to José María's comments, but he let them go, because one thing was certain: no need to start a fight when it would be so much easier to throw him out without further discussion. He contented himself with grabbing José María by the arm and pulling him aside from the rest, just far enough to talk to him without being overheard.

"Listen here, stupid, I made a joke, so don't take it like that, 'cause I have a temper too," he warned him.

"Well, well: I'd never have known."

"Known what?"

"Doesn't matter, let it drop. If you've got a temper, we'll let it go."

"Are you being insolent with me? Don't you realize that I could throw you out right now if I felt like it?"

José María nodded his head in silence, without taking his eyes off the man for an instant. For his part, the foreman held his gaze without relinquishing his grip. Worse still: the pressure on José María's arm grew as the two stared at each other, chiming with the increasing imminence of a physical reaction on José María's side.

The foreman was certain the young lad was ready to attack him at any moment: he imagined him grabbing the joist beneath which they stood with both hands then swinging up to throttle him with his legs. He had seen him do just that a few weeks earlier, when José María was joking about with a mate of his, and he'd been

impressed by his agility. José María spat sideways and said:

"Let's get back to work, we're wasting daylight…"

The foreman was reluctantly obliged to let him go.

José María went off to get changed. The weather remained heavy and this mood was echoed by the attitude of those who had been closely watching the scene, and even of all those who had only recently come on site. As soon as they got to work they knew something was up. Nobody said anything as they moved around slowly, staring down at the ground, blinking less than normal.

"Just see what an umbrella can do," muttered one in a low voice.

"Nothing to do with the umbrella, everything to do with the joke," responded another. "You need to know who you're dealing with. That María is just as dangerous with or without the umbrella."

Everyone called him María, just like that. It was something that occurred naturally, and which José María didn't seem to mind about one way or the other. In actual fact he couldn't have cared less. Even Rosa began to call him María. There was something in his viscerally taut body, together with the length of his eyelashes, which almost automatically ruled out the possibility of his simply being called José. You only needed to see him to realize that his agility was a truly exceptional gift, and, this being clear, this threat of danger meant that people called him "María" with caution, as if, despite his willingness to be called by that name, they were still wary of causing offence.

It made the foreman's blood freeze to have María outstaring him, despite his naturally sanguine nature. Only now the episode was over and done with did it begin to make his blood boil. Such sudden changes in temperature had prevented him from being properly aware of how dangerous María was. The same thing as happened with the doorman. If the two men had paid a little more attention, they wouldn't have tangled with him. María had done nothing to them; it was they who had picked on him. No doubt a warning signal following some kind of natural law becomes activated, prompting the spider, even before becoming hungry, to trap its little flies, but there was no proper reason to count Rosa in among their number.

It had happened without the foreman and the doorman noticing, and it was what so blinded Rosa: she was a dutiful and even-tempered girl, her head filled with endless dreams. María's dangerous edge, which Rosa chose to put down to his "character" (as when she called him "pig-headed" or "stubborn"), made him her ideal foil, the complementary and hitherto missing piece in her make-up. She felt charmed to be in his company. She thought herself protected, and was under the impression that the two of them together could conquer the world. It was an image so far outside reality, she never noticed the time passing when they were together.

María would stop by and see her daily at six thirty in the evening, at the end of his day's work. They met at the tradesmen's entrance to the mansion, and between one kiss and the next they laid their plans – all endowed with an astounding triviality, but fundamental to their relationship – things like meeting up the next day at the Disco supermarket or spending Saturday night together in the small hotel down on the Bajo.

Rosa and María made love every Saturday, and spent all their Sundays together. They would have made love every day if it were down to them, since Rosa was free to leave the house whenever she wanted, but to tell the truth they lacked the money. They both earned the same amount: 700 pesos a month. Two hours in the hotel cost twenty-five pesos, which means they spent a hundred pesos a month simply on making love on Saturday afternoons, and 200 if they stayed on Sundays too. They went Dutch (first him then the next time her), but Rosa's monthly outgoings were far less than María's, given that he had to make the daily journey from home in the Capilla del Señor, a round trip which came to another 260 pesos per month. So, on sex and travel he was paying out 310 pesos each month. Had this been the sum total, they could have lived comfortably on the remaining 390 pesos, but María was also a human being who required food and cigarettes and (on those rare occasions when he tried to be a gentleman as well as a normal person) liked to pay for an occasional beer or a coffee on their excursions to the city centre, all of which left him precious little choice beyond restricting his lovemaking to Saturday afternoons.

Rosa might have lamented the fact, but it was true that she didn't live within the same financial constraints as María. Better still, Rosa was in a position to make savings. Her food was provided, as was a roof over her head, and she wasn't required to travel anywhere. She didn't even need to buy clothes – although nor did María, if the truth were told. Buying magazines didn't come into it: her boss Señor Blinder had a subscription to *Selections from the Reader's Digest*, which arrived punctually by post, and which she opened and read, sometimes even before he did.

To María, earning exactly the same as Rosa was slightly worrying, since it seemed to him he was obliged to make considerably greater efforts than she ever did. This was doubtless so in matters requiring physical strength, less so in terms of the amount of time he dedicated to his job. In that sense at least, Rosa worked twice as hard as he. But time was not taken into account by the purely physical mentality of María, who had no money even to buy a haircut. So it was that he wore his hair extremely short above the ears and rather longer down the back of his neck, not because the cut was in fashion but because it was one he could do himself in front of a mirror.

Alongside the developing relationship with Rosa, his "attitude" problems made him a long series of enemies in the neighbourhood, some of them occasional or erratic, others well-established. For a start, the doorman, now reinforced by Israel, who was the son of the president of the Owners' Association. Israel looked like a twenty-six-year-old rugby fan, bulkily built, with the eyes and mouth of a frog, and a head buried between his shoulders. Yet he'd never played rugby, had no idea even of the basic rules – though he always went out dressed in shirts belonging to any or every team in the world; he sweated heavily too, which smelled really badly, so he smothered himself in extremely expensive perfumes which, when they combined with his personal odours, generated a unique and almost intolerable aroma, to such a degree that most people were compelled to hold their noses.

He always went about dressed in jeans and chamois moccasins and – it's now perhaps worth mentioning – he was a Nazi. The doorman had phoned to tell him about the encounter with María because he knew that Israel loathed foreigners, the more so if they happened to be poor, and worst of all if they wanted to act sharp in his neighbourhood. He had said as much to the man himself on more than one occasion: "Let me get my hands on him and you'll soon see…" It was his favourite turn of phrase, especially so when he could use it to close a conversation. Very well, now was his opportunity to put his words into action. Posted at the building's entrance and keeping company with the doorman, he was waiting for María to pass by. Israel flexed the joints in his fingers, then his wrists, ankles and neck, while the doorman chain-smoked one cigarette after the next.

María came by at six thirty on the dot, just like the previous evening. The doorman saw him coming and nudged Israel, indicating the man with his chin.

"That's him."

"Back off," Israel muttered under his breath.

The doorman took a step backwards.

Once again, the climate looked ominous. María, oblivious to the possibility of getting caught out, came along whistling a merry and mellifluous melody, pure birdsong; he had the bag containing his work clothes slung over his shoulder. As he drew level and was about to pass the two men, one of them – Israel – cut in front of him, rudely blocking his way.

"Where are you going?" he asked him.

"Why?"

"What d'you mean, why? Because I'm asking you, you Black Jewish motherfucker."

María looked at the doorman, engaged in cleaning his nails with a key, and understood the source of the problem. Next he acted entirely out of character: taking the bag off his shoulder, he set off at a lick, heading for the corner. He ran with such speed and agility that Israel hadn't yet turned around before María had disappeared from the scene.

"Did you see that?" Israel asked the porter.

"I told you he was swift."

"What kind of a cowardly motherfucking Black Jew?…
Those Bolivians are all the same…"

"He doesn't seem like a Bolivian to me. Tall, for a start."

"Chilean?"

"Maybe Peruvian…"

"Peruvians are also motherfucking Black Jews – and
dwarfs to boot. But this one's a Chilean. If he's not a
Bolivian, definitely a Chilean. What's more I'm gonna
get him. I'm gonna force that motherfucking Black Jew
Chilean to swallow the Malvinas whole!"

As he said this he crossed himself, loudly kissing his
thumb at the end. No sooner done than he began
chewing his thumbnail.

He couldn't believe it. Nor could the doorman. The
pair of them were equally astonished: they'd never seen
anything like it. He was the world champion of cowardice.
Between María's cowardice and his speed, neither Israel
nor the doorman could tell which surprised them most.

At that moment, María reappeared. First Israel spotted
him, rounding the corner and heading towards them.
This time he came accompanied by Rosa.

"Is that him coming this way again, or is there something the matter with my eyesight?" enquired Israel.

"Yup – it's that motherfucking coward!" exclaimed
the doorman. "Mind you it takes balls to come back this
way… even more so with that girl on his arm!"

"Move back."

"Let's leave it for tomorrow, Israel… the girl's bound to
start screaming and attracting attention… I'll risk losing
my job over the fuss…"

"Nobody's going to put you out of a job. My old man's
president of the Owners' Association. Step back and I'll
take over…"

"Does it bug you if I go inside?"

Israel wasn't answering. He had his eyes fixed on María, now barely twenty yards away. The doorman hesitated an instant (he wanted to stay, he wanted to watch him destroy the guy), but in the end he opted to protect his job, and went inside the building.

Israel stopped in the middle of the pavement.

Rosa realized something was up and became anxious. She said nothing, but María felt her clutch his arm more tightly.

"Calm down," he said. "It's some idiot with nothing better to do. Carry on walking as if nothing's up."

Israel planted himself in their path.

"Ohh…" murmured Rosa, as if sighing. She was more bemused than frightened.

Israel addressed her first: "You're the maid at the Blinder household, aren't you?"

Rosa nodded.

Israel swivelled his gaze towards María in order to address him next, when he felt a sudden blow smashing his nose up between his eyes. He backed off, lifting a hand to his face. When his hand fell back it was dripping blood. María leaped forwards and unleashed a headbutt to his forehead, along with a follow-up punch, this time to the stomach. Israel let out a groan, his legs buckled beneath him, and he wove from side to side, finally managing to reach out an arm and prop himself up against a wall. María and Rosa carried on walking.

"Let's go, darling."

Israel collapsed into a sitting position on the threshold of the building. He left the bloody imprint of his hand on the wall behind him.

The doorman, who had witnessed everything, emerged from the building, his eyes round with wonder.

"Police!… Police!…" he started shouting.

But Israel, using the last vestiges of energy remaining to him, yanked at his leg and said, his vanity still intact:

"Don't wake sleeping dogs, you idiot, can't you see what state I'm in? Help me inside…"

The doorman took him by the arm, supporting him until Israel managed to scramble to his feet, then brought him into his office, closing the door.

Over the following days, every time Rosa left the mansion to go to the Disco supermarket, she crossed to the pavement opposite and avoided passing in front of the building, for fear of coming face to face with Israel. Not that she actually saw him again, but she was obliged to pass the doorman more than once, and he followed her with his gaze, as if to say "I'm going to get you". She told María about this.

"Don't let it worry you. It's nothing to do with you, it's all my problem."

Always, whether coming or going from the Disco Supermarket, Rosa made a short detour by the construction site, just to catch sight of María for a minute: there she could hear the racket of the machines, the blows of the pile-driver, the scraping of spades in buckets, everything slowing down, as if the film of reality was slipping in its reel. Rosa wasn't pretty, but she shone with the glow of a million good intentions, a light which set off her physical virtues. Her love for María was so obvious that, on leaving his workplace, the machines, hammers and spades reverted to their usual rhythm with excessive application, as if in a rage. Just for an instant, the noise was deafening.

At the end of winter, Señor and Señora Blinder went on holiday to Costa Rica. Rosa remained alone in the house. The Blinders' departure signalled the (provisional) end of the absolute control of finances over sexual activity: from then on Rosa admitted María into the kitchen to make love. Now they could make love on a daily basis, not only on Saturday. So they made love twice a day, morning and evening. In addition, Rosa could make him a meal, which María would call in to collect from the house early in the morning: most often an escalope with potatoes – fried potatoes, roast potatoes, mashed potatoes. They ate a lot of escalopes and potatoes. That afternoon, she was waiting for him with two escalopes and a bottle of wine. They ate together, and María left the house as night was falling.

There was an absolute ban on bringing outsiders into the house. Rosa knew the rule, of course (before leaving, the Blinders had reminded her twice over, each time with a fixed stare), but she was so utterly besotted with María that admitting him into her kitchen was the lesser evil. In any case, she was cautious: she mounted a real smokescreen in front of the neighbours; at times she'd dally in conversation with María at the grille by the tradesman's entrance for a long while before letting him into the house as soon as she was entirely confident that no one was watching; sometimes she went outside to greet him with a rake in her hand, as though María were the gardener... As soon as he was inside, they ate, made love (only in the kitchen) and watched television on a miniature set which Rosa brought down from her bedroom and put on the dining table.

The first time María came into the house he was surprised by its size.

"All this is the kitchen?" he enquired. "It's bigger than my house!"

The second time he came indoors, he tried to poke his nose in upstairs, but Rosa prevented him with a daft plea ("Don't compromise my position!" she begged) and he didn't insist. He let three or four days go by. Then Rosa gave in and took him upstairs to her bedroom.

He followed her down a dimly lit corridor to a small and poorly ventilated bedroom with an unmade bed and a lamp without a shade on the bedside table. María was astonished: he couldn't believe that anywhere inside the villa could be so narrow and dark. While they were making love, Rosa explained to him, in terms that would get the discussion over with once and for all, that this was the service wing, which even she didn't know from end to end; the rest of the villa was quite different. Then she asked him to hang on a minute, and went to the bathroom. When she came out, María was no longer in her room. Rosa went into the corridor, calling him in a low voice, as if she were afraid the Blinders could hear her.

She continued on to the end of the passageway. Then she retraced her steps and ran to the kitchen. María wasn't there either. Rosa became alarmed, agitated, as if what happened later had already taken place. It seemed she was running from one end of the house to the other in a desperate search for him, until she reached the corridor that led to the living room – a spacious lounge, with all its windows tightly shut – where she at last could hear María calling her. Yes, it was definitely him calling her.

"Rosa…"

"Yes, it's me. Where are you?"

"Rosa?" asked María, whispering from somewhere unseen.

"Here I am, María! Come out, please, don't play games!"

"Where are you, Rosa?"

"Here! And you?"

Rosa heard the sound of something suddenly falling and breaking.

"Where *are* you, María?"

"I don't know, Rosa. I'm lost... I can hear but I can't see you..."

She found him in the library. Rosa switched on the light. María was standing stock-still at the desk, one hand resting on the back of Señor Blinder's favourite chair. In the darkness, he had knocked over a standing lamp; the light had fallen onto a settle and the light bulb and its glass shade had shattered. The carpet was covered in shards of glass, as if the lamp had multiplied itself in the fall.

Rosa skewered him with a look. Then, as though afraid to let him go anywhere alone again, even to the kitchen to find a dustpan and brush, she grabbed an art-exhibition catalogue from on top of the desk and used it to sweep up the glass fragments.

"I went to take a quick look around and things got complicated..." María confessed. "I came down the staircase, took a turning down a passage and then... Well, you know how this whole house is a labyrinth."

"I told you to stay in the room."

"Don't get cross," said María, lifting the lamp stand up off the floor. "I didn't put a light on because... just imagine if someone were to see you..."

"And who would that be, if there's nobody else in the house?"

Rosa said nothing more. She rose and, closely followed by María, went to the kitchen to throw the broken glass into the rubbish. It was a real shame: they'd frittered away their time and now it was getting late, and Rosa was in a bad mood. Señora Blinder would reproach her for having broken the glass lampshade – she might even deduct the cost from her wages. María collapsed into apologies and excuses, each time extending a hand towards Rosa's cheek, but she kept on brushing it away like a fly. Finally, María removed a piece of the glass from the rubbish bin and assured Rosa that the next day he would buy her another identical shade. Rosa clicked her tongue and opened the kitchen door to accompany him out to the pavement. María jammed the door with his foot and Rosa permitted him to kiss her goodnight. Then she went to the tradesman's entrance giving onto the street. She looked to left and right and, when she was certain there was no one else around, signalled to María to come out. Once at the grille, he kissed her again.

"I'll come by tomorrow…" He said. "And again, please forgive me. Bye, beautiful."

"Hi, beautiful," was the first thing he had said to her the next day. It was so cold that when Rosa embraced him, he could feel the cool of her hands through his jumper. He didn't have the lampshade with him.

"I was just listening to the radio and heard that there was an impressive tornado over Costa Rica," she said, "only I'm not certain whether they said Costa Rica or Puerto Rico…"

"There are loads of tornadoes in the United States…"

"But they didn't say a thing about the United States, they only mentioned Costa Rica or Puerto Rico, I can't remember which. Apparently the roofs of the houses blew away. And they said the boats broke their moorings and scooted about in the air like flying ducks…"

"What if one of those yachts landed on your head? Can you imagine that?"

"I don't want to imagine it… How cold it's got!"

"Freezing. Though I don't feel it myself."

"I prepared this for you," said Rosa, holding out the plastic box she gave him each morning. "You have two chicken legs, and I also included some mashed potato…"

"Thank you, darling. Well, I'd better be off now, it's already gone eight o'clock…"

"Did you get home all right last night?"

"Perfectly. How was your night?"

"I fell asleep immediately."

"Didn't you watch the TV?"

"Yes, but there wasn't anything on. I switched it off and I'd no sooner put my head on the pillow than I was asleep. Oh – and I added some red pepper to your lunchbox, to spice up your potatoes."

"You always make them so tasty…"

"Time to be on your way, you don't want to be getting there late."

"I'll see you after work."

María gave her a kiss, winked and set off on his walk to work.

Up until this point, everything had followed its normal path. But the problems started as soon as María got to work. He bumped into Israel and the doorman, on their way back from talking to his foreman. Israel and the doorman passed by without looking at him, then carried on walking, hastening their pace.

"María," the foreman called out, "come over here a second, I need to speak to you."

The foreman walked away from his workers in order to speak to María alone. He leaned one foot on the floor and a thigh against the edge of some scaffolding. María was standing beside him, but the foreman took his time in withdrawing a packet of cigarettes from his shirt pocket, raising one to his lips, then patting down his trouser and anorak pockets in search of matches, before finally asking:

"Do you have a light?"

"I don't smoke."

"Ricciardi!" he called out.

Ricciardi pushed his way past them carrying a sack of cement.

"Ricciardi, give me a light."

Ricciardi approached them, still with the sack of cement on his shoulder. Using sign language, he indicated he had a box of matches in his back trouser pocket. The sack was so heavy he didn't have the necessary strength left even to open his mouth.

The foreman felt his pockets with a degree of apprehension, but failed to find what he was looking for, so Ricciardi had to turn around to proffer him the other back pocket. The foreman repeated the operation without finding any matches.

"See that? You're just doing it because you want me to put my hand down your trousers, aren't you?" he announced to everyone.

Ricciardi cracked a smile through clenched teeth and planted himself in front of the foreman so that he could try his luck with the front pockets. At the final try, the foreman tapped on a box.

"Here they are," he said.

But before inserting his hand inside Ricciardi's pocket, he scrutinized him carefully. The two men stared at one another in silence for at least an endless split second, bearing in mind that this was a delicate body zone to investigate by hand. Afterwards – long afterwards, it seemed – the foreman carefully introduced his hand into Ricciardi's pocket and with the tips of his fingers extracted a box of condoms, which he then hastily and immediately attempted to shove back inside.

"What the fuck is this, Ricciardi? Do you or don't you have a light?"

Ricciardi made a peculiar gesture, a gesture that might have been a shrug of the shoulders, had it not been for the sack that was weighing them down. The foreman told him to move on and Ricciardi immediately set off, his back bowed ever lower as he wove an increasingly erratic path. The foreman once more found himself alone with María.

"Some gentlemen came to see me. They say you're going about causing trouble in the neighbourhood…" he told him.

María stared at him in silence.

The foreman continued:

"They mentioned that you called one of them an idiot and you punched the other one in the nose. Is all this true, María?"

"Yes," replied María calmly.

"And you can confirm it just like that?"

"How would you like me to confirm it, then?"

"I don't know. Tell me in your own words."

"Yes, I'm telling you, yes. One of them is an idiot and I hit the other one."

"So why did you provoke them?"

"Me? I didn't provoke anyone. They came looking for me."

"It seems they found you," remarked the foreman, with heavy irony.

"Yes."

The foreman gazed at him, chewing on his unlit cigarette.

"Quit fucking about, María. Are you going to tell me that I also came looking for you? Because you know I've never come looking for you, but the other day I almost hit you... you, you piece of shit. So don't come talking nonsense to me."

"What did you call me?"

"What did I call you when?"

"What did you call me just now?"

"When?"

"Just now."

"What did I say?"

"That's what I'm asking you. Why don't you repeat what you said?"

"And what was it I said to you?"

"Say it again, you."

"Don't address me as 'you' like that. I'm 'sir' to you. Tell me what it was I called you, and address me respectfully. Are we clear?"

"Didn't you call me 'a piece of shit'?"

"Can't remember. Perhaps I did. I can't recall it now, but I could have done so, and quite right too. Who the fuck do you think you are, to go around insulting people? Where the fuck do you think you were born? What on earth do you think it does for me, the foreman on this site, when the neighbours start turning up to inform me that you're running around causing a scandal in the district? And d'you want me to tell you another thing? Yes, I called you a piece of shit. Why not? Do you have a problem with that?"

"No..."

"Ah, so no problem there?"

"No."

"Why, you a faggot?"

"Yes."

"Look at you."

"Why, you want to fuck me, you?"

"I told you not to keep calling me 'you'. On top of which, you got here late this morning, it's already ten past eight. You're sacked. For causing a disturbance in the neighbourhood, for turning up late, for addressing me as 'you' instead of 'sir', and for being a faggot. Take your things and get the fuck out of here."

María picked up his belongings and left.

3

That day he came around to the house a half-hour later than usual. Rosa brought him into the kitchen: the escalopes were ready, fresh from the stove. There was also a dish containing a mountain of fried potatoes piled on a paper serviette, and a bottle of white wine. María hung his bag on the back of a chair and sat down at table.

"I cooked them in the oven this time," Rosa said as she put an escalope on his plate. "It's the first time I've done them this way. For myself at least: the Señora always requires me to make them like that for her. But for myself, I've never done them this way before. Let's see how you like them! How did it go at work today?"

"Fine," answered María.

He cut off a slice of escalope and lifted it to his lips on a fork.

"It's good," he commented, chewing. "Why don't you put on the TV?"

"Oh, right – I'd totally forgotten! What's the time? On Chiche Gelblung's programme at seven o'clock they're going to have that little dwarf, he's only eighteen inches high. Do you remember what I'm talking about?"

"No."

Rose had switched on the television and was flicking through the channels on the remote control, searching for Channel 9.

"I saw him the other day on *Hola Susana*, and apparently they're going to invite him back on again today. I don't want to miss it. He's no more than eighteen inches tall, something so... Ah, here we are. Well, maybe not, this is Chiche... perhaps he'll explain what's coming up."

Rosa sat down facing María and ate the first half of her escalope in silence, without taking her eyes off the screen. Chiche Gelblung was practically rubbing his hands with glee and begging all those watching the screen not to look away, since any minute they would be able to see the smallest man in the world. Next came the commercial break. Rosa served María with fried potatoes, and then herself.

"Poor little thing," she said, "you should have seen him. He barely even came up to Susana's knees... Is anything up with you?"

"No. Why?"

"You're very quiet..."

"I've only just got here."

"I know you've only just arrived, but you could still say something, couldn't you?"

"I'm fine."

María poured himself a glass of wine and downed it in one. Then he refilled his glass and, as an afterthought, poured Rosa a glass too. He was dying of thirst. As he drank the second glass and set about serving himself a third, he realized that two days must have gone by since he'd had a drop of liquid to drink.

"Do you have any soda?" he asked.

Rosa said she did, rose from her chair, and went to the fridge. She took out a bottle of soda and put it on the table. María knocked back two glasses filled to the brim, the first one mixed with wine.

"What a thirst you have!" said Rosa.

"Did you see that? It must be the dust I swallow every day at work... On top of which I've only just noticed that it must be two days since I drank anything."

"Anything?"

"The same thing would happen when I was a boy. I could go for two, three or four days without having a drink and then, all of a sudden, I'd have to catch up. I'd drink anything, including orange juice I squeezed myself. I'd crush the oranges in my hand... crush them to a pulp... or I'd pierce a hole in one and suck out the juice... Lots of kids did that back in my village... There was only one little shop and that was ages away, and in any case no one had so much as a peso. We would pretend we were drinking soda pop! Ah well, why don't you say something?"

"Where was it you were born?"

"In Gobernador Castro."

"I don't know it..."

"Why would you expect to? It's a shit hole, and it's down near Ramallo. Does that name mean anything to you?"

"No..."

"Ramallo's another shitty dump. I don't really know how to describe where it is... It's about sixty miles from Rosario, a bit more towards San Pedro. If you know San Pedro and from there..."

"What, on the other side of Rosario?"

"No, before Rosario. On this side, and before you even get to Ramallo, maybe thirty miles before. Heading towards Rosario, about thirty miles down the road from here. Gobernador Castro is around a hundred and ten miles away."

"Ah…" murmured Rosa, attempting to decipher the mass of information.

"Yes," confirmed María.

"I thought you were born in Capilla…"

"Nope. I moved there when I was quite young, but no. I was born in Castro. Mother of God, how my hand is hurting…"

"What happened, did you bang it?"

"Yes, I sprained it."

"You banged it or you sprained it?"

"I banged it."

"And so how did you sprain it?"

"I dunno. Must have banged it lifting something. At the moment I can't rightly remember, but right now it's hurting all over."

"Here, help yourself to another escalope. Would you like me to slice it for you?"

"No, leave it. I'll do it myself."

"I feel embarrassed to tell you, but… last night I dreamed about you. You were riding on a white horse, with a sword in your hand…"

"You were dreaming about St Martin…"

"No, seriously. You were riding naked."

"Bareskin?"

"Yes, bare to the balls…"

"Bareskin, I'm telling you, and mounted bareback."

"Oh, all right, I'm sorry! Look what you're making me say…" she blushed. "You were riding this horse stark naked, sword in hand. And the sword and your… well… prick, and the horse's neck, everything was full of nerves and veins… I swear I woke up at that point…"

"Have you always had erotic dreams?"

"No. The night before last I dreamed I went window-shopping. I went crazy looking in those shop windows, and I went into a boutique and bought a heap of clothes and then I went to a hairdresser and had highlights put in my hair."

There was a silence while Rosa gazed at him.

"Are you certain nothing has happened?"

María shook his head and Rosa didn't persist. They had maintained their conversation while keeping an eye on the Chiche Gelblung programme, to spot whether the dwarf put in an appearance. But the presenter had moved on to another category of deformities by now, one in which there was no chance that dwarfs might be included, even though the dwarf was still being trailed at every commercial break. Before the final section, when he was due to sign off, Gelblung started to apologize for the fact that his time had run out, and to promise a special programme the next day, entirely dedicated to the smallest man in the world. But Rosa became annoyed and switched off the television before Gelblung finished making his promises, and went to sit on María's lap. She threw her arms around his neck.

"Do you know what I like best of all about you?" she asked him.

María shook his head.

"You seem such a mystery. So quiet... It's as though you're always keeping something back..."

She moved to kiss him on the lips. But less than an inch before touching him, she paused, stopping in mid-air as if frozen, her pupils open wide, and her eyes fixed on the street outside.

"What's up?" asked María.

Rosa shut him up with a rapid "shshsh".

She jumped down from his lap and ran to the window.

"Oh my God!"

"What's up?"

"It's the Señor and Señora! They're opening the door! Mother of God! Now what do I do? If they catch you here they'll flay me alive!"

María went over to look out of the window. Rosa was right: a man was stooped over the door lock, trying to insert a key. Beside him stood a woman. The woman was just about to ring the bell.

"Listen to me and calm down, I know what we need to do. Rosa, listen, and stay still a moment... breathe deeply... I'll hide myself away here, behind the dresser. You open up to them, they'll come inside, and I'll take the keys and leave, then push them back to you through the grille by the garden gate. It's easy. Breathe deeply, you need to be able to pretend with conviction. If they notice you're nervous, they'll take you and shake everything out of you, down to the dream you've just told me. Breathe. That's it... Well done... Now I'll go and hide and you go and open the door..."

"What about the dishes?" hissed Rosa.

"I'll sort that out; you open up. Do they usually come into the kitchen first thing when they arrive?"

"They never arrive at the tradesmen's entrance. I can't think what could have happened!"

"They must have lost the keys to the front door."

"Possibly... Oh my God, they were supposed to come back next week!..."

"Do you see? That tornado you were talking about must have struck..."

The bell went on ringing, ever more insistently. María pushed Rosa towards the door. Then he grabbed his plate and shoved it into the dishwasher, and hid himself behind the dresser.

Rosa reappeared with Señor and Señora Blinder, carrying their suitcases. The Señora asked why she'd taken so long to answer the door. Rosa explained that she'd been upstairs in her bedroom tidying up. Señor Blinder pushed open the kitchen door and lost himself in the depths of the house, silent and ill-tempered.

4

One of the first things to catch his attention was the sharpness with which the street sounds penetrated the house; at certain hours of the night you could even hear the scratch of a dog's toenails on the pavement. As he set about exploring the interior of the house, he recalled his surprise at discovering how small its interior really was, compared with how it looked from outside. It seemed the more so because there weren't that many pieces of furniture or ornaments, and because from the outside you could take the whole thing in at a glance, something impossible to achieve when you were indoors.

He had installed himself on the top floor, in the attic, where he *felt* himself to be more invisible. The first night, he didn't sleep at all. The second night, for fear of someone coming in, he slept underneath the bed. The key stayed in the lock, but it took another day before he decided he could close the door and remove the key: if for some reason somebody came to the room and found the door locked, presumably they'd assume that someone else inside the house had left it locked up; they'd look for the key, and when they didn't find it, they'd either call a locksmith or else they'd simply abandon the attempt to get inside. What would they come looking for inside this room anyway? There was nothing there apart from a bed with an old mattress and an empty wardrobe.

Even so, for the first nights he spent in the house, he took fewer precautions than Rosa did when she first started working there. For Rosa, despite having received a catalogue of obligations and prohibitions which one way or another took care of her working and leisure hours, ended up feeling lost, diminished, often frightened. But once she'd learned where to find the floor polish or the ironing board, or in which drawer the Señor kept his socks or the Señora her blouses, she felt more at ease, increasingly comfortable with the domestic routines into which she gradually became integrated.

Two years had gone by since she first came to the villa. During that whole time, she had never done anything untoward. A few days after the Blinders' unexpected return, her personality began to change: she became taciturn, distracted, went everywhere bright-eyed, on the brink of tears, wringing her hands. She had received no further news of María at all.

Three days had gone by since the Tuesday, during which she heard nothing of María. On the Wednesday she waited with an escalope sandwich: she thought of going out onto the pavement to give it to him wrapped in greaseproof paper, so he could eat it on the bus. Now that the Blinders were back, her meetings with María would have to revert to being restricted to the tradesmen's entrance. But María didn't appear. Rosa guessed he must have been a bit nervous as a result of the Blinders' sudden return, the fact that they'd been on the point of surprising them there together, and supposed that must have been the reason for his few days' delay in coming to see her again. He didn't appear on Thursday either. Rosa began to get worried.

Her assumption that María would like to leave a couple of days' pause before coming to see her again could by now only apply to this last day.

On Friday, she stopped by the building site on her way back from the Disco supermarket. Someone told her he wasn't there, that he hadn't come in for the past few days. She realized the atmosphere seemed charged, but she couldn't tell why.

She was on the point of leaving, when an unskilled worker, on his way in with a bucket of sand, approached and told her that María had been thrown out of his job.

"What? When?"

"On Tuesday."

"I didn't know anything about it… what do you mean, he got thrown out?"

"Yes, he got the sack."

"He didn't tell me…"

"Sorry," replied the builder, as he continued on with his bucket: the new foreman had come out of a portable toilet and lit a cigarette, then stared at her through the smoke, with the hungry look of a wild beast.

That afternoon the police came to see her. There were two of them: a tall one with a black moustache as stiff and straight as a toothbrush, and a young one with long hair, both in plain clothes. They spoke to her in the main entrance. They asked her a thousand questions about María. They wanted to know where he lived, his phone number, if he had been with her on the Tuesday. She told them he lived in Capilla del Señor, and didn't have a phone number. Yes, he had been with her the previous Tuesday. Had anything happened to him?

"It would seem that the earth has swallowed him up," said the moustache, with heavy irony.

46

Rosa was bereft. She was relieved that neither the Señor nor the Señora were home at the time, for although they always spoke respectfully of the police, they disliked the idea of having them around. A few years ago the police had killed a burglar just outside the house, and had blocked off the pavement, where they remained for over an hour, until they finally decided to remove the body. In the interim, one of the policemen rang the bell, asking for a glass of water... Señora Blinder took his request as indicative of a scandal, since there were a dozen more appropriate houses to call on along the block, more suitable to involve in satisfying a basic need such as that for a drink of water. Years had gone by, and from time to time Señora Blinder would still mention the matter of the policeman's thirst. The Señora would clearly never forgive Rosa if the police came to the house to discuss her boyfriend with her.

But why were they looking for him? What on earth had happened to María? Where on earth was he?

Worst of all, she had no one to talk to, no one in whom she could confide her worries. OK, fine, so they had sacked him from his job, and it appeared he hadn't wished to inform her of the fact, but that wasn't a sufficient reason simply to disappear. Could he be ill? Maybe so, and perhaps that was the likeliest explanation. If he weren't ill, why would he just disappear? Wasn't it obvious to him that, if the cause of his disappearance were the shame of losing his job, at any moment she would be bound to show up at his workplace to enquire after what had happened to him, and would then be informed of what had actually occurred? He had to be ill.

She wasn't mistaken: María was running a temperature. Stretched out on the mattress in the room he had

47

made his own, he was shivering with cold. Hours had gone by since he'd last made a move. The index and middle fingers on his left hand were still wrapped in a cobweb which he'd unintentionally leaned on that morning, when he got up to go to the toilet. He was weak. Even turning onto his side on the bed required a major effort; also, although the mattress was of superior quality, an old coil-spring number, the bed's wooden slats creaked and he was afraid someone would hear, which meant he had to remain there utterly immobile for hours on end. In addition to which, two days had gone by without him eating a thing. The venetian blinds in the room were down and, if it weren't for the sounds from downstairs, he would have had no idea whether it were night or day.

As soon as he began to feel a little better, he returned to the bathroom. He had found the toilet the previous night, in a courageous and very daring excursion, reconnoitering the terrain across a large part of the attic floor. Even the bathroom looked abandoned, just like the room in which he'd installed himself. It was clean enough (Rosa must have been wiping it down from time to time), but it was obviously out of use. He took advantage of his expedition to try the doors of the rooms along the passage: most he found locked, others gave onto more empty spaces, and one was employed as a sort of loft or store in which all kinds of junk was heaped, from old clothes to plastic bags to children's toys.

Getting himself up and going to take a leak was a whole new adventure. He left the bedroom door open, just as he'd found it, so that anyone who suddenly decided to come upstairs wouldn't notice any difference, assuming such a thing were possible, and also in order to be able to listen out and have enough time to go and hide, should it prove necessary. The principal problem arose when it came to pulling the chain, an operation which required a considerable amount of time; the cistern was ancient, and the water tank located at a distance from the bowl and inserted in the angle between the wall and the roof, from which dangled a chain ending in a wooden handle which he would lower an inch at a time, until the first trickles of water began to flow downwards. These little trickles, amounting to no more than a small leak, María caught and used to wash his face, and did so with such care than not even he could hear a sound.

Incredibly, sometimes a drop of water would break away from the main flow and plink on the edge of the bowl, or else he himself might, while urinating, wet the edge of the seat, which he would then need to cautiously wipe clean (with a piece of paper, or with his shirt tail) before leaving the bathroom.

Up until Thursday night, when he decided to venture into the kitchen, he had stayed entirely in his room, except when making his occasional forays to the bathroom, or his one and only investigation of the attic floor. He hadn't moved anything, nor left the slightest trace of his presence there: every item was properly in its place.

His fever was so high that he spent the first few days lying on the bed; he had put his work clothes on over his street wear, covering himself with a pair of trousers and even with his rucksack, but he was still shivering. The cold weather of early spring combined with the cold atmosphere in the house and the cold shivers of his fever. Yet he never for an instant considered leaving his hideout. On the contrary: he needed to stay there to recover, and to do that he needed to find food.

Thursday night he went downstairs to the kitchen. The villa was arranged on four floors, and he wasn't certain even as to how high up he was, but he reached the kitchen far more quickly than he'd anticipated. He went barefoot, having left his shoes in the rucksack under the bed. Some parts of the house were in total darkness and he could see nothing at all; other rooms admitted moonlight from the garden through odd openings, or else the light of the garden lamp, permanently left on, penetrated some part of the building and allowed him to see where he was going. Not that this left him feeling any more secure. After all, what could he see? Nothing but pictures, mirrors, carpets.

The wall clock over the kitchen door showed three o'clock in the morning. He opened the fridge: the light hurt his eyes and made him blink. He quickly shut it again. What would he possibly remove without Rosa noticing something missing when she came down the next morning? On the floor, beside the chair, he saw a plastic bag which had split a moment beforehand, and was still coming apart and unfolding like a flower. He grabbed it and started opening it: it was a Disco supermarket bag and made a frightening amount of noise. María exploited the sound of a passing car to rip it open. Then he filled the bag with some bread he found on the sideboard, before opening the fridge door again and helping himself to a little of everything inside it, without paying overmuch attention to what he took.

On turning to leave, he glanced at the clock again: it wasn't three in the morning but half-past midnight. He had spent fifteen minutes in the kitchen: the clock must have been showing a quarter-past twelve rather than three o'clock when he arrived. He was shocked: it was too early to have come downstairs, someone in the house might still be awake. He left the kitchen, every muscle tensed, more alert than ever, and mounted the service stairs two or three steps at a time.

He paused for breath on the first floor. He could feel his heart pound beneath his hand. He needed to get to the end of the corridor, to get to the other staircase and climb the last two floors to reach the attic. He resumed his steps, but halfway along he heard a faint and half-choked sobbing in the dark. He paused, more than anything afraid of suddenly bumping into the person who was crying, then backed off a few paces, before suddenly noticing that the sobbing came from the room opposite where he had shrunk back, and he carefully applied his ear to the door. It was Rosa. She cried with her face buried in her pillow: a muffled weeping, heart-rending but stifled, suddenly interrupted when María leaned his ear on the keyhole.

Two seconds later, Rosa put her head outside the bedroom door and looked down the corridor. The lamp on her bedside table outlined her like a silhouette. There was nobody there. Rosa blew her nose and went back into her room.

At that precise moment María, his forehead on fire and his feet freezing, was sidling up the staircase towards the attic. Once back in his room and eating his food, he thought – with a degree of logic – that Rosa was burying her head in her pillow for fear of being heard. On top of which, she had actually gone into a spare room to have a cry. Or had she been there on some errand or other, and suddenly found herself in floods of tears? There was another question even more important than this one: was Rosa's own room really so near to that of the Blinders that she would need to muffle her tears in a cushion? No. Rosa slept in the east wing and the

Blinders in the north wing of the first floor. But María wouldn't figure this out for another couple of days. For the time being – and including the following day – he would, unwittingly, be waiting to learn, and from the lips of Señora Blinder herself, that the police had been there looking for him.

Next morning, he awoke feeling much better. His meal had consisted of no more than a bread roll, five olives, a slice of raw ham, half an onion (likewise raw) and an apple. He was awoken by the street sounds outside, spreading like a mirage through the silence within the house, or perhaps merging with it. However long had he been there? Three days and two nights, he estimated. Or maybe four days and three nights. Lying still in a foetal position on the bed, he thought it must be about time he left. Then, when he rose from the bed, he entertained the possibility of staying a little longer, perhaps one more day. Where could he go? There was absolutely nowhere he could go and hide...

He was no longer running a temperature, although his bones and his joints were aching somewhat. He observed the door to his room did not make the slightest sound, even if he yanked it open to test it, just as he had when he returned to his lair.

He emerged onto a landing flooded with a dangerous light, but for the first time he could at least get an all-round view of where he was. He surveyed all of it slowly, mentally noting the arrangement of rooms and passageways, and the position of any object he might have collided with on his previous ventures, or might conceivably collide with on any future excursion.

He descended a floor. If the attic looked uninhabited, the third floor gave the impression of being a temporary dwelling; maybe this was where the Blinders accommodated their house guests, if they ever had any. Every window was closed, but all the rooms had the necessary creature comforts: deep-pile carpets, a chimney nook, a little trolley loaded with alcoholic drinks, a shelf laden with books, a phone, a television set... The beds were not made up, they were bare of sheets and covered just with a bedspread, and the atmosphere in these rooms was dry and fresh, as if someone came in and gave them a daily airing. Here and there on the walls there were portraits of serious-looking men and women done in oils, each with a gilt frame. The main staircase descended almost to the main chimney breast. María proceeded in the opposite direction, following a corridor leading to the service wing, along which he passed a number of empty rooms of much smaller size: these belonged to the house staff, who years ago must have been a full complement of servants, from butler to housekeeper. Why, then, did Rosa sleep on the ground floor and not upstairs here?

As he descended further, he realized the entire house had been reorganized as a result of the reduction in the number of its inhabitants. The room occupied by Rosa must, for example, have originally been used by the housekeeper or head butler. The facilities on the second floor were very similar to those on the third, although the decoration was much heavier, almost baroque in style. The living room contained a remarkable number of tables, side tables, settles, sofas and easy chairs.

He approached a table covered with framed photographs, and leaned over each one in turn to study it more closely. Each one was a portrait of a blonde woman, aged around forty, always wearing the same smile, although the hairstyle kept altering. At times she appeared alone, and at others she was accompanied by a man of about the same age: presumably either her husband or her brother. The were other men of around thirty-five to forty-five years old and lots of small, blond, smiling or serious children of various ages and in various places – anywhere from in a church to on a beach. One of the men appeared in just one photograph and by himself: even his photo frame seemed to occupy the least important place on the table. In the last photograph María examined, everyone appeared together (with the exception of the man of whom only one portrait was exhibited), one linked to the other behind a gentleman and lady seated on cane chairs, both dressed up to the nines… At that moment he overheard a rasping voice up on the first floor. He went over to the staircase.

Señora Blinder had just learned of the visit from the police. Israel had stopped her on the street a few minutes earlier and, maliciously, had expressed his concern about "the case of Rosa's boyfriend". Alarmed, Señora Blinder raised a hand to her mouth.

"My God, Rosa, it looks as if your lover killed some-one!"

Rosa's knees collapsed under her. Her head was spinning.

"They say he killed the foreman on the site where he worked! How long is it since you last saw him? Why didn't you tell me the police had been round here? Rosa, are you listening to me?"

"It can't be…"

Rosa began to cry.

"Now what are we going to do? Everyone in this district is already gossiping about it. How long is it since you saw him?"

"Three or four days," answered Rosa.

"Why didn't you inform me the police had been round?"

"I got scared, Señora…"

"The police come round to *my* house to see *me*, and you don't tell me anything about it?"

"I was afraid, Señora…"

"Unbelievable. What am I going to do with you?"

"Forgive me Señora, please. I didn't know anything."

"You didn't know anything about what?"

"Anything about anything, Señora."

"What a shock, you going out with a murderer! He would come to see you and you'd open the door to him…" she went on. "I saw him on two or three occasions, at least in the distance, and didn't like the look of him. That's how he looked to me at least. So now what?"

"Now, I don't know, Señora. I think it's impossible, there must have been some mistake…"

"And you're telling me you never saw him again?"

Rosa swore on the cross of her closed fingers. Then she began crying again.

"So why didn't you see him again? Did he tell you something of what he'd done?"

"No, Señora."

"Didn't you know anything at all about it?"

"Nothing at all, Señora."

"Are you sure?"

"Yes, Señora, but it can't possibly be true. He's incapable of swatting a fly, he's such a good man, he is…"

Señora Blinder paused a moment in silence, her head swirling with conflicting notions. Finally she seemed to banish them all; she uttered a deep sigh, and she left the room at a smart pace. Rosa sat down on the edge of an armchair and buried her face in her hands. María withdrew and began pensively to climb the staircase.

5

By the end of the second week he knew every sound in the house, much as if he'd always lived there. Something similar would also apply to the space and the position of objects within it, essential to his survival there. Concerning the noises he himself made, there remained something of his initial fear, however unjustified it had become, but which it was difficult to shed. For example, certain doors took more time to open than strictly necessary: he would open each one inch at a time, even when he understood that were it to creak, it still wouldn't be heard by anyone else. Even when asleep, he would only change his position in bed with extreme caution.

His precautions, combined with his natural agility, meant that he moved about in the gloom with the ease of a ghost. More than a ghost, in fact, he resembled a figure out of a silent film projected outwards from the screen, an image already familiar with distances, provided with an extraordinary radar, which at moments of distraction – like when he was about to knock a flower vase flying, or trip over the edge of a carpet – sharpened his extra-sensory perception, allowing him to dematerialize or dissolve.

He knew he couldn't relax his guard to the point where he affected the slightest detail in the way in which things were positioned around the house. He was aware that nobody would notice whether a pair of scissors or the bathroom towel were in the same place as last week, but he paid scrupulous attention to leaving everything precisely as he found it. From time to time he would awaken suddenly in the middle of the night, and run out of his room in order to shut the bathroom door, which he had absent-mindedly left open, but on the whole he made no mistakes: he carried a detailed and exhaustive inventory of the place and position of every single object around in his head, and was scrupulous in respecting them, by now almost unconsciously.

In addition, his inventory had to be revised from top to bottom, on a regular basis: from time to time upstairs in the attic, weekly on the second and third floors, and daily down on the first floor and in the kitchen, following Rosa's cleaning rota around the house. The ground floor remained an utterly unknown territory to him. He avoided it: every night, he descended to the kitchen down the service staircase. He was absolutely certain that this way he wouldn't meet a soul, least of all Señor or Señora Blinder. In return, he could bet his life that neither Blinder had ever set foot in his part of the house. And every night, on his way down, he would pause an instant outside the door to Rosa's room. On the whole he would hear nothing, since he only went downstairs so very late at night, but occasionally he'd hear her cough, or walk up and down in a fit of insomnia, tidying up her room, or watching television. Once he overheard her masturbating.

He missed her. On more than one occasion, he considered the possibility of revealing himself to her, but he didn't dare believe that Rosa's love of him would reach such heights. She'd be scared, then no doubt decide he was mad. It would have put her in an impossible position, too difficult either to accept or assimilate, most of all in coming to terms with the fact that he was the principal suspect of a serious crime.

He started having imaginary conversations with Rosa. To begin with, they were brief dialogues, of the "question and answer" variety, generally involving people or situations of the most boring ordinariness. Later, when he had finally accepted that Rosa was not to blame for his inability to admit to her that he was in hiding there, and permanently eliminated the thought of making her his accomplice, the dialogues became longer and more amiable. He spoke often with her while he ate or while he read, or occasionally even when curled up near the window, as close as possible to fresh air and light, just to get a bit of warmth on his face.

In the second-floor library there were hundreds of books of every kind, from adventure novels to medical texts. María would lock the door to his room, cover the crack at the bottom of his door with his shirt, then switch on the night light and read until he fell asleep. Sometimes he needed to flick back through the pages and reread a passage again, since he had really spent the time in an imaginary argument with Rosa, while his eyes followed the lines on the page inattentively. It came to his attention that he had never seen Rosa reading, despite the quantity of books in the house. In her spare time, she never did anything except watch television.

"It's because reading is harder work than watching television," she told him.

"Why? All you need to read is to sit or lie down, just like when you're watching television."

"But you need to use your brain."

"That's a lie! You can read perfectly well without thinking at all."

Rosa masturbated often. Not during the early weeks of his disappearance, while she was distraught, but from the time when she seemed to accept that María wasn't going to come back. In one of his mental discussions with her, María "understood" that Rosa still loved him, even though she now no longer held out any hope of seeing him again. Rosa told him she did not consider him capable of killing a fly, and he kissed her silently, then, without letting her go from his embrace, explained that on that day, when the Blinders came home, he did exactly what he told her he would: he waited for the Blinders to come indoors, he came out of his kitchen hiding place, then opened the gate onto the street, before realizing he had no idea where to go, so he closed the gate again, leaving the key in the lock, as if someone had opened it from outside, and went back into the house.

"What do you mean, you had nowhere to go?" Rosa asked. "Why didn't you go home?"

"Home, Rosa... I got on really badly with my foreman. Nobody would believe me if I said I wasn't the one who killed him... The police would've come to my house looking for me; I'd be in prison now, who knows how long for. I'd prefer to spend the rest of my life here."

Silence.

"I love you," Rosa said, and dissolved into thin air.

She masturbated thinking of him. And he took to spying on her. Rosa masturbated in her room or in the bathroom, any time between ten o'clock at night and one o'clock in the morning, almost daily. (On one occasion María caught her masturbating at dinner time, having just served the Blinders their soup, and just before they would call her to serve the main course.)

Masturbation occupied a good part of Rosa's free time, almost as much as watching television. She could spend an hour or more just on foreplay; she would even sometimes start playing with herself in the bathroom, in the shower, then finish off in the bedroom. María, his eye glued to the keyhole, would masturbate in rhythm with her. He was intrigued by the variety of techniques and utensils Rosa employed. On occasions she'd soap and caress herself until the foam took on the consistency of cream; then she'd seize a bottle of deodorant with a rounded head, crouch down in the bath, turn on the shower (María couldn't quite keep her in sight, however hard he tried) and insert the end of the bottle between her legs as the water beat down on her back, rinsing her off. Sometimes she'd do no more than sit over the spout on the bidet, without even pausing to remove her clothes, her pants tugged down around her ankles and her uniform apron hurriedly hoiked up, as if she had almost no time for all this.

María thought often of Rosa's effrontery. The first time they had ever made love, in that hotel down on the Bajo, Rosa had already behaved in a way utterly strange to him, with a total and unexpected abandon. María had been to bed with many whores in his life (and he'd also had previous experiences with so-called virgins), but no one had ever offered him the combination of ardour and innocence that Rosa presented. Everything was permitted, from the most gentle tenderness to the most degraded lasciviousness.

Rosa took such delight in sex that she could cause him sudden consternation. She'd crack jokes, as if sex were above all else a joke; she'd unexpectedly poke his balls with her finger, or grab his cock and work it back and forth as if it were a car gearstick, going so far as to make engine noises with her mouth. And she'd laugh like an (adorable) idiot when María held her down by her wrists and glowered fiercely at her.

So he wasn't at all surprised when he found Rosa masturbating so often. What did seem strange to him was that sometimes they'd reach orgasm in unison, each of them on their own side of the door. At which point María would hurriedly depart, holding one hand cupped... A moment later, Rosa would emerge from the bathroom, go into her room and start watching television. María would wipe his hand underneath his pillow, and lie on his back for hours, thinking of her. It was this or prison. There wasn't really that much to think about after all.

6

He established a routine of gym exercises. Stretches, flexes, stomach crunches, squats, the works. His abdomen, already naturally muscular, now resembled a washboard. He had doubled the strength in his arms. Working out was now the only form of physical exertion he had undertaken since incarcerating himself in the house; it became essential to him to maintain his routine, partly because his body was now the only tool he had to work with. He cultivated every muscle in his body as carefully as if it were a magnolia.

You could say that reading, masturbating and working out "in his spare time" could sound like a load of nonsense, but the premises were perfectly reasonable: he genuinely had to work hard in order simply to eat and fulfil his basic biological needs. These were the activities that consumed most of his day. It was an adventure to go up and down from the attic to the kitchen in order to steal something to eat: on every trip he played Russian roulette with life and liberty. To be able to do it, he had to learn to have complete control of himself and of his environment.

Before ever going downstairs, he would do breathing exercises in order to obtain the necessary degree of relaxation; this would last for only a few minutes, before his state of heightened alertness would reappear, and then return renewed at every step. His excursions to the bathroom or the third-floor library were equally risky, as were the "leisure walks" he undertook. On the latter occasions, he would lean over the banister of the first-floor stairwell, to see if he could hear the sound of voices on the ground floor, while he picked his teeth with a straw taken from a broom, or basked in a moment of sunlight from the adjacent window. But basically he felt little anxiety over having nothing to do: he now lived outside any system of production and he enjoyed the lack of demands on his time. He was answerable to no one, he had no orders to follow, and his one and only worry was to remain out of sight and remain undiscovered.

In fact, the adrenalin rush arising from the risky situations in which he could find himself gave him a degree of pleasure, giving him the sensation that even a vital necessity was transformed into an adventure… Take washing, by way of example. He had now spent nearly three weeks in the house without washing. Formerly, whether at work or at home, he took a daily shower; here it was unthinkable. Yet he still had to find a way of keeping clean; his entire body was itching, to the point where some nights he could scarcely sleep.

The central heating system only had radiators on the ground and first floors. Still, the second floor remained more or less warm thanks to the fact that warm air rises; by the third floor the air was cooler, and in the attic it was freezing. He decided to wash himself in one of the downstairs toilets. That night, as every night, he obtained his supper from the kitchen, took it up to his room, then descended the flight of stairs to the bathroom in the north wing (done out in black marble, coated in lime scale). He stripped off, got into the bathtub, wet the sponge, and rubbed himself from top to toe. The water was icy, and he'd been unable to find a bar of soap anywhere, but once he'd finished, he felt much better: shivering but renewed.

He wiped out the bath using the sponge, then put it back where he had found it, dressed and went back up to his room. A minute later, as he was eating, he realized that he hadn't the faintest idea what day it was. He simply hadn't kept daily tally. This realization left him feeling somewhat lost. As of that night, he vowed to keep track of the days. He had murdered the foreman on Tuesday 26th – or was it the 27th? – September. He estimated he had spent at least twenty days in the house, which made it now around the 13th or 14th October. The next day, he stole a pencil and a sheet of paper, to keep a record.

He ate a chicken leg, a roll and a tomato, before flinging himself onto his back on the bed, arms akimbo under the coverlet. Without emotion, he considered the fact that three days after killing the foreman, he should have been in receipt of his fortnight's wage packet (also of the fact that on the same day he had left his Rolex hanging from a nail in the work hut) when he was suddenly aware of a noise in the room. He froze to the spot.

For an instant, he considered the possibility he might have moved one of his legs without being conscious of doing so, and it was therefore him making a noise. But then he swiftly noticed that the sounds were coming from over by the door. He became alarmed, still frozen in position. Perhaps there was someone on the other side of the door. He heard the sound again. It sounded most like the noise made by someone turning the pages of a book, one after another. Most probably Señor or Señora Blinder had come upstairs to look for a book, or an old notebook, in the loft and, whichever of the two it was, had paused there to leaf through the book just outside his door. He decided to get up and listen more closely: it was something inside his room.

It must have been two or three in the morning. He opened the blinds a crack and by the street lights he could see a rat, running to hide underneath the cupboard. María stopped stock-still, his hand on the blind, thinking. How had it got in? Maybe he hadn't properly shut the door when he went to get washed, and the rat had found a way into the room. He closed the blind, opened the door ajar, knelt down beside the cupboard, and gently patted the floor with the palm of his hand. But the rat didn't make a move until María rolled up his pair of trousers and, as if he were wielding a whip, directed a couple of blows to the bottom of the cupboard.

Then the rat emerged from its hiding place, running everywhere as hard as it could, but it didn't head for the door; it made a couple of laps round the bed, went behind María, and hid itself again under the cupboard. It was a gigantic rat, the size of a man's shoe. And it was petrified.

María repeated the operation. He saw it come out. This time it didn't look quite as big, but was even faster. María stayed another minute on his knees beside the cupboard, looking and listening. Nothing. Finally he gave up, shut the door, and went back to bed. Let the rat do what it will.

Later that night, properly clean and no longer hungry, he recognized that at least he now had time to think. And the first thought he had was that he had never thought before. The next minute he was soundly asleep.

7

The next morning, when he returned from the bathroom carrying a glass of water to prepare his maté herb tea, he noticed the door of his room was wide open. His blood froze in his veins. He retreated across the loft, ten or a dozen yards in front of the door to his room. From this position he could see Rosa opening the window. She wasn't wearing her maid's uniform: instead she was in jeans and a T-shirt, with a cloth thrown over one shoulder. A vacuum cleaner stood in the doorway.

He felt as if all was lost. He had made the mistake of leaving the room without taking his bag with him – as he always did, except when he went out at night. The bag was underneath the bed, and as soon as Rosa started vacuuming there, she would be bound to discover it. That wasn't even the worst of it: he'd left a book lying on the floor too. Not to mention the bone from his chicken leg!

He had to prevent Rosa from running the vacuum cleaner under the bed. For now, she was still busy with cleaning the windows. María didn't think twice about it: he left the loft and ran on tiptoes over to the vacuum cleaner, removed the adaptor from its socket, and returned to his place in the loft again. He had barely got back to base before Rosa left the bedroom.

If Rosa had had the least suspicion that María was hiding somewhere in the villa, she would have to have spotted him then. Clearly she did not. Instead she picked up the vacuum cleaner and took it into the room without registering what had passed before her eyes for a fraction of a second: a hand holding the door jamb at the edge of the loft, and the profile of a face with one eye glued to her and what she was doing.

María was as breathless as a long-distance sprinter and his heart was pounding heavily. As he attempted to steady his breathing, he saw Rosa emerge from the room once more, looking about her to see if she could find something there on the landing floor... His scheme had worked. Rosa felt around in her trouser pockets, shrugged her shoulders, and set off downstairs in search of another adaptor. María slipped back into his room. The book he'd abandoned on one side of the bed now lay on top of it, so he decided it was better not to move it; obviously Rosa must have picked it up from the floor and placed it there, without paying it any heed. He took his bag out from under the bed, but couldn't see the chicken bone anywhere at all. He crouched, searching more and more desperately, here there and everywhere, thinking that Rosa must have trodden on it without noticing. He simply couldn't find it. Then he heard Rosa's voice saying:

"Here I am, Señora, up here, cleaning!"

Silence.

"Yes, Señora, straight away!" Rosa replied, and this time her voice sounded much closer than before.

María had no more time to continue looking for his bone. He left the room and hurried into the loft. He went inside, closing the door after him, leaned his back up against a wall, then let himself slide down it until he was sitting on the floor, clutching his rucksack to his chest. A moment later he changed position, or perhaps, more accurately, his attitude altered: he set the rucksack to one side and let himself slide still further, this time from drama into slumber. He imagined that Rosa had found the bone, that she had reported it to Señora Blinder, and that two or three policemen had come up to the attic and conducted an inch-by-inch search until they discovered him. No sooner had they done so than they clamped him in handcuffs and dragged him downstairs.

On the landing on the first floor Señor Blinder, there waiting for him, immediately blocked his way and started punching him, without any of the policemen attempting to prevent him. He passed Señora Blinder on the ground floor, who backed off while staring him in the eyes. Rosa huddled in the doorway giving onto the street, silently shaking her head, her face wet with tears. Señor Blinder stopped them suddenly:

"Not that way," he said. "Take him out through this door," and he pointed at the tradesmen's entrance.

Rosa was obliged to go with them. She went ahead and throughout her ordeal kept turning back at every step, as if she couldn't believe what she saw.

"Why?" she asked him.

"How do I know?" he answered. "I could give you so many reasons... Are you well?"

"Why?" repeated Rosa.

He shrugged his shoulders. She opened the tradesmen's gate and let them through. In the second before they put him in the police patrol car, Rosa succeeded in asking him, tender as a mother:

"What have you been eating?"

He emerged from his daydream when the water in his jug ran out.

The maté tea was his best acquisition in recent weeks. The truth was it was the same as a morning cup of coffee;

he had found a number of maté gourds in a kitchen drawer, and he was sure that nobody would notice if one were missing. Rosa drank maté daily, so there was always an open packet of the tea lying around. For now, María had to drink his maté cold, although soon he would begin to heat up the water... He emerged from his dream at this point, and realized that this whole time he'd not heard a single sound emerge from the vacuum cleaner. He awoke properly and looked out at his room. The door was shut tight.

Was Rosa still in there? It seemed highly unlikely that Rosa would shut herself in there in order to clean. Surely she must have finished the job and left. Just in case, he decided to hang on a little longer before returning to his room. He occupied himself by going through some of the boxes stacked up in the loft, which seemed to be filled with anything from straw hats to old crockery. Quite a lot of the stuff up there could prove useful to him, should occasion arise. He had already sniffed around inside a few of the cases, coming across various old shawls and blankets, and a mother-of-pearl card box with a deck of playing cards inside it (with which he'd played solitaire), but it was only now that he noticed the walkman. Manufactured by Sony, it had probably once belonged to one of the Blinder children, or possibly grandchildren. It didn't have any batteries, and although he searched high and low, he couldn't find the headphones. He decided to take it with him in any case. He put it in his bag and, for a brief instant, felt as if he were in the midst of a shipwreck, a Robinson Crusoe rescuing from what was left of his sea voyage whatever might prove useful to him. It was time to leave the loft behind him. He zipped up his bag and set off to return to his island.

The air inside his room now seemed fresh and new. The book still lay on the bed. While María had been in the loft, he had waited every moment for Rosa to discover the chicken bone and, beside herself, go and show it to Señora Blinder. Presumably the truth was that she had not found it at all. Otherwise – as it was a "bone of recent provenance" that no one could believe was some old thing brought there and forgotten who knows when and by whom – his dream would have become reality. So the first thing he did on getting back into his room was to search for the bone, going back and forth on his knees, criss-crossing the room. But he was just as unable to find it as she was.

He decided to open the window. It was a good opportunity, given that Rosa had been there only minutes earlier, and could always assume she had failed to close the thing properly. Light flooded into the room as María peered outside. The sky looked uncertain whether to clear or to cloud over. The citizens' habits appeared to be running to form for the time of day: he estimated it must be around two in the afternoon. On the building site, his former workmates must be just about finishing their lunch break. Was there anything about that world outside he still missed? A good roast beef. Three days earlier he had eaten it straight from the oven. And a cigarette. He had never smoked heavily, but ten yards below him, down on the pavement, he saw a man pass by with a cigarette between his lips and he longed to have one. That was when he realized that what he most missed was using his sense of smell. To be able to smell a roast, inhale a cigarette. And the scent of Rosa.

Ever since he'd been living in the villa, he'd smelled nothing except the odour of damp. Did Señor or Señora Blinder smoke? In the villa, cooking took place both at midday and again in the evening, yet the smell of it never penetrated as far as his upstairs attic. Why would they, then, be able to sniff out the smell of his tobacco, had he any? He determined to undertake a reconnoitre, on one of the very next evenings, down to the living room on the ground floor, with the intention of finding out whether Señor or Señora Blinder were smokers and, assuming that one of them was, rob them of one or two of their cigarettes. In his own room, perhaps anywhere on the top floor, he could smoke without fear of discovery. Maybe he could even try it out right next to the window, open just a crack, looking out on the street, just like now.

He spent the afternoon reading. When the daylight began to give out, he did his gymnastics exercises. Then he went to the bathroom, washed, and returned to bed to take his siesta. At two in the morning, he went downstairs to the kitchen to get his dinner and, bearing in mind that Rosa gave no sign of having noticed any change in the quantity of food there, decided to help himself to breakfast as well. That way he ate better and risked less.

After dining, he set off on his walk around the house. He undertook it completely naked. He'd decided henceforth to leave his rucksack in the loft, where it would be hard to distinguish from the mass of other bags and boxes, and in order not to have to carry it around with him wherever he went. He had learned to move about in such a stealthy fashion that he seemed almost motionless, or as if the floor itself were transporting him. Like a man on a moving walkway. The same thing applied when he did his athletics. He didn't jump like a ballet dancer, in the sense of becoming suspended in mid-air, but did the opposite: he took large leaps, allowing the weight of his body to catapult him in a long jump, just above floor level. He was capable of jumping more than three yards from his starting point, virtually without having lifted off. At the end of the leap, one of his feet would just skim the floor's surface, in order to kick off on the next leg of his trajectory. His body thus described a succession of interconnected curves, each one propelled forwards by sheer force.

He returned an hour later. The window into his room was still open. The sky was clear, and cars passed only intermittently; there were no pedestrians. The moon shone like a radioactive rock. He lay down. He was about to fall asleep when he heard some faint noises from on top of the cupboard. He refrained from moving. It didn't even seem to matter to him that the rat hadn't emerged, that it was, after all that had happened, still in his room. Now he knew where the bone had gone.

"Goodnight," he said to the rat.

He heard himself and was shocked. It was a long time since he'd listened to the sound of his own voice.

8

One evening he heard "new" voices inside the house. Leaning over the second-floor banister, he could catch intermittent glimpses of a man in a dark suit and a woman who, from his vantage point, seemed to consist in little else but a bright yellow wig balanced on the points of two stiletto shoes which came and went almost hysterically beneath full white skirts, and which made her appear like an energetic fried egg. The date was 30th October, and it was Señora Blinder's birthday. María couldn't manage to overhear exactly what Señora Blinder was celebrating, but he did manage to gather that the new visitor's name was Rita, and that the couple were perhaps the Blinders' only close friends.

Rosa went back and forth, in and out of María's field of vision, carrying trays of canapés. She made the trip with frustrating frequency, as if instructed only to serve one canapé at a time, no doubt annoying and interrupting the guests as well, in spite of the fact that their voices couldn't have sounded more cheery.

At a given moment, everyone vanished; Rosa went into the kitchen and the Blinders, together with their guests, went to take their places at the dining table. María managed to catch odd snatches of conversation, before he began to hear retching sounds coming from behind him. He retreated to an alcove which looked out onto the avenue, and opened the window. A young – or at least relatively young – man was vomiting outside the front door to the villa.

He closed the pane and, as if the pane were the view-finder of a camera, ran the image past his retina again: there could be no doubt, the man was the same as the only photo of a stranger on the table of family portraits. The bell began ringing insistently.

Intrigued, María crept down to the first floor. The tone of the mutual greeting was kept to one of welcome and false conviviality.

"Álvaro!..." said the father.

"How did you get here?" enquired the mother.

"Sit down..." (The father.)

"Have you eaten?" (The mother.)

"See, I remembered it after all." (Álvaro.) "Many happy returns... Doctor... Sara... how are you? Hi there, old man. I promise I'll bring you your present tomorrow, Mum. And what about Peru, Doctor, have they decided? Are we selling them arms or not?"

"Álvaro, please…" (The mother.)

They then spent over an hour discussing football. Nothing could interest María less than football. In any case, he stayed put just to listen in on the conversation: he was hardly ready to leave the party just because the topic they were chatting about didn't interest him overmuch; he didn't get that many opportunities to listen in on something that, while phoney, at least sounded agreeable.

It was obvious that the alcohol was flowing. The voices… their subjects… even the silences… had grown denser. Someone had put on a CD. How long had it actually been since music played in that house? María had never heard as much as a single chord, not even from a neighbouring villa. He had the impression that this was the first time in generations that music had made itself heard here. He had already drawn his own conclusions as to what kind of people the Blinders were, so the wholly unlikely and inappropriate sounds now emanating (from a CD by Cristian Castro) confirmed his assumption that music was about as relevant to the Blinders as literature to a boxer. It wasn't even one of their discs: it belonged to Rosa.

María repeated with the CD what he'd done with the conversation: he stopped to listen to it. The difference between the two was that whereas the topic of football hadn't interested him in the least, at least he really liked Cristian Castro's songs. Better still: if he weren't mistaken, he himself had made a present of that very CD to Rosa. At least, he was sure he'd given her a disc by Cristian Castro, but he hadn't had time to copy it before giving it to her – nor, as a result of all that had happened, to listen to it on his own, when he got in from work – so he couldn't be entirely certain whether or not this was the same one. The fact of the matter was that Cristian Castro's voice caused him to drop his guard, even to drop off to sleep.

This was when something extraordinary happened.

(This isn't what follows. What follows is merely an infidelity.)

Made drowsy as he was by the music, María didn't notice that Señora Blinder had escaped from the table, or from the dinner party, still less from the dining room, and that she'd just hooked up with her male guest halfway up the staircase, in the shadows.

There was nothing in principle to suggest, from the attitudes adopted by either party, that the two of them were lovers. Quite the opposite, in fact: it was evident that they had been good friends for many years, to the point where they had almost nothing left to tell one another, but it was also plain that they were fed up with longing for each other in secret. Desire and its repression were such a powerful force between them that when they met halfway upstairs (one going up and the other coming down), it was as if they were strangers.

When María had realized how close they were to him, he had moved back. Now he decided to advance a little again. He couldn't see them, but he could hear them absolutely clearly.

She gave the impression of being somewhat agonized.

"All of a sudden, I felt such a vast emptiness, so very vast, that it made me feel as if I was entirely swallowed up by it," Rita Blinder was saying. "I don't know if that makes it like a religious experience, most likely it does. I feel as if I exude the symptoms of religious withdrawal. First I feel utterly empty, then utterly filled, but with a longing to enter a retreat. I keep thinking of something which Epictetus said... you do know who Epictetus is, don't you?"

A silence.

María visualized the man nodding vaguely.

"Epictetus," Rita Blinder went on, "said that when God is no longer able to supply us with faith, or love, or anything else, he gives us a sign of retreat. He just opens the door and invites you in with: 'Come'. And you reply: 'Where to?' Then He tells you: 'Nowhere in particular. Only back to where you have come from, to things you warm towards and places you have an affinity for, back to the elements.'"

Another silence.

María imagined Señora Blinder fixing the man with her gaze, anticipating some kind of a response from him. He could as good as see the man casting about desperately for something to say. He could hear the man clear his throat.

Finally he heard him say:

"Sometimes I think I know everything, and at others nothing. My dearest, this is one of those occasions when I feel I know nothing. Believe me. The honest truth is that I don't know what to say to you."

There was a pause and then what followed was a deep sigh, emanating from Señora Blinder. She sucked air into her lungs as if her head had only just surfaced above the water – and she started to descend the staircase. The man, despite the fact she had met him on his way up, followed her down.

That was when María heard the sound of shattering glass. He looked right, towards the stairs going down to the service wing, from where the noise had reached him as if echoing from a tomb. He followed the sound, and heard a slam, the sounds of a struggle, then the sound of another slam. Again, silence. María was now on the bottom step of the service stairs, at the start of the corridor. He leaned his face forwards and Álvaro just entered his line of vision.

The door to Rosa's room stood open. Álvaro, his back turned towards María, was propping himself up against the wall with one shoulder. He was struggling to unstick the shoulder but his legs weren't helping. In fact, his knees were buckling. Finally he managed to achieve lift-off and, making the most of his sudden success, he zigzagged his way to the kitchen, where another struggle erupted.

María could hear Rosa's voice saying:

"Álvaro, enough. Stop!"

"Come here a minute… Just a little minute…"

"Leave me alone!"

"Don't be naughty…"

María didn't dare to approach any closer to spy inside the kitchen, but it was hardly necessary: Álvaro was bent on abusing Rosa, that much was obvious. He clenched his fists. He even tightened his toes against the edge of the step. What could he do if Rosa didn't manage to get the guy off her? Had he already abused her previously, abused her, his girlfriend, on previous occasions?

Rosa left the kitchen, smoothing down her uniform, and ran to the end of the passage, where she hid herself behind a door. Álvaro came out a second later.

"Rosa!" he called.

His feet described a large circle, and the rest of him followed in a surprisingly straight line behind Rosa, as if he were bent on drawing the outline of a helium balloon on the floor.

María remained rooted to the spot, paralysed with rage. Then he returned upstairs again, in order to take up his position above the living room, but although the music had stopped, he couldn't hear anyone inside talking; he leaned forwards again to get a better look and saw Rosa setting off in the direction of the kitchen carrying a tray. An instant later he saw her again. This time Rosa was bearing four glasses on the tray (rather than five, leaving him to think that Álvaro had been excluded from the toast), along with a bottle of brandy. María could hear her leaving the room.

He went up to the second floor, ran into the east wing, and peered between the curtains and through one of the windows looking out onto the garden. The Blinders and their friends were seated around a little white table; Rosa deposited the glasses on the table and went back indoors. No sign at all of Álvaro.

He came across him a short while later, purely by chance. When passing one of the bedroom doors on his way back to his attic, he heard snoring. He thought that whoever was inside must have seen him on the way back to his room: until just a few minutes ago, he had been almost next to the bedroom. Then he looked inside. Álvaro was sleeping face down on the bed, fully dressed, down to his shoes and tie. He gave the impression of having collapsed there.

María had killed his foreman without any feeling of rage. If you wanted to put it better, you could say he had done it in the memory of his rage, some hours after having experienced it, as if the rage itself had vanished, only to leave him in the hands of the new form of reason it had engendered. It was wholly premeditated. Not in detail, nor in method – those remained free to be improvised on the spur of the moment – but in its ultimate objective of killing the foreman. When the time came, he paced the outskirts of the work site,

77

leaving and returning to it more than once: he took his time. At half-past six, or possibly a few minutes later, once he was certain he would find the man alone – the foreman always being the last to depart – he went in. He was feeling calm. He hadn't even bothered with an alibi. He had no thought of possible consequences. The foreman had: he looked into María's eyes and knew that this was the last man he would ever see.

The terror which followed this realization froze him to the spot. He didn't even have time to swallow the saliva rising in his throat. María thought that Álvaro, even drunk and asleep – maybe just because of this – would probably offer more resistance than the foreman. In addition to which, this time he had no stone in his hand, as he'd had wielded on the previous occasion. He would be obliged to strangle him, or... To his right he caught sight of a poker. He estimated that two or three blows would be enough to smash his skull. He could visualize the entire scene: the first blow... the second, to the forehead... the blood... And suddenly he felt overwhelmed with tiredness, as if he'd already executed the deed.

He left the room and slowly crossed the dark landing, heading in the direction of the staircase. Halfway over he heard a noise. He turned to look. One window pane, which had swung itself shut, was swinging slowly open again... It was the wind, nothing but the wind. Even so, he hastened his pace.

9

Spring only really arrived in mid-November. Outside – he could observe it in the garden or on the street – it had begun earlier, before you could get a sense of it inside the house. The attic and the third floor stayed damp and dark, but all the same the temperature had risen in there by at least a degree a day in recent weeks, until finally it seemed on a par with that outside.

María had come to feel more comfortable and at ease: he slept somewhat easier, food seemed to taste better, he allowed himself longer in the shower... Even his daily constitutionals around the house lasted longer. This was helped by the fact that his confidence had also improved: neither Álvaro nor the police had re-appeared, Señor and Señora Blinder were spending more and more daylight hours away from the house, and María's domination of its second and third floors was nearly complete, in every sense. For some time now, he'd been able to tell the footsteps of the house's inhabitants apart; now he'd learned to distinguish the direction they were heading in, their degree of haste, even what each person had in mind as they went on their way. He knew their routines, their caprices, he had the measure of their breathing and differentiated the manner in which they opened and closed doors – and he could tell who had just deposited their glass on the table... all learned as a blind man would, since he had never – or almost never – seen any of them.

Two or three times he had gone into the Blinders' bedroom, so at least he'd obtained a physical portrait and an intellectual profile of the two of them. He had investigated their wardrobes, and always noted the new copy of *Reader's Digest* on Señor Blinder's bedside table, and the daily paper on the Señora's, invariably with a glass of whisky standing on it. Rita Blinder drank in bed, and no doubt in all kinds of other quiet places, like her son. And finally he discovered that a man had started phoning Rosa.

This discovery coincided with another, which he made through his passion for intercepting all forms of communication with Rosa. The very thought of Rosa kissing another man wounded him deeply. In a fit of jealousy, one afternoon when Rosa had just received one of these calls, María raced up the staircase and picked up the telephone on the third floor. But he could only hear the dial tone through it. He headed downstairs again at full speed. Rosa was still talking. That meant the house had to have two phone lines.

At that moment, he wasn't particularly bothered with following Rosa's conversation, with its suggestive giggles in the background. His only thought was that he must have made an extraordinary discovery. "I've got a phone!" he told himself. It was so absurd it was emotionally moving. He could speak to Rosa, he could ring and talk to her without her suspecting he was no more than a few yards away.

He went back up to the third floor, picked up the telephone directory and searched for a phone number under the name Blinder. There were seven.

He began with the first. He dialled the number, and while the phone rang at the other end, he realized he hadn't the faintest idea what he was going to say. He cut the line. He had let himself be carried away on an impulse, but – wasn't it perhaps something he should think about? He made an effort and thought.

He felt a dizziness throughout his body. A dizziness that didn't – as usually happened – begin in his head. Then he picked up the handset again and resumed dialling the first number on the list.

Engaged.

He hung up and redialled.

Still engaged. He couldn't believe it. He was no more than two steps away from his lover and all he got was: engaged!

The line stayed engaged for at least another half-hour or more. He was inclined to keep trying (after all, he had all the time in the world: there had never been a man more absorbed in what he was doing and with so much time to be doing it), but he heard the sound of the street door opening, and the voices of Señor and Señora Blinder as they came inside, arguing. So he put away the directory and the handset (it was a free-standing one, a half-moon of transparent plastic, with all the internal chips and cables exposed, some apparatus which seemed to have been dropped there from another planet) and took it to his room with him.

He closed the door and resumed dialling once more.

This time the phone rang.

(Brilliant.)

The phone rang seven times before it was picked up, and a woman's voice spoke:

"Hello?..."

María cut it short and hung up.

It hadn't sounded like Rosa's voice. "OK," he said to himself, "I don't even know if I'm really calling home or not." After all, it might not have been "his" Blinders' home number. Had he been lucky enough to get it right first time, the only way to be sure was to ask for Rosa by name, and to be allowed to speak to her. So he redialled yet again.

While the phone was ringing, he asked himself what on earth he'd say if Señora Blinder happened to answer...

This time the woman picked it up at the second ring, before he'd had a chance to gather his thoughts.

"Good afternoon," he said, faltering. "Please may I speak to Rosa?"

"Rosa who?"

He put the receiver down.

It wasn't her.

He felt relieved that it was the wrong number, so irrationally and profoundly relieved that he frantically dialled the next number, as though he'd suddenly realized that his relationship with this telephone would be sufficient once and for all to modify his entire genetic make-up.

Another woman responded this time.

"Good afternoon. Please may I speak to Rosa?"

"Who is it?"

"A friend… one of Rosa's friends. Is she in?"

"There's nobody called Rosa here…"

He hung up again.

Then he dialled the next number.

"Good afternoon. Is Rosa there?"

"You've got the wrong number." Yet another woman.

It seemed to him as if that night there had to be some reason why all the Blinders in town were next to their telephones. So he went on to the next number listed.

As the phone rang, he suddenly felt as if he were immersed in a world of irrationality and chance. He had crossed his legs, as he always used to before settling himself in at home in order to listen to the lottery results on the radio. Even now, he could feel the palpitations…

"Hello?"

Yet another woman on the line.

"Hello?" she repeated.

María paused. It was her! It was Rosa!

Impatiently, Rosa hung up.

María dialled the number again.

He dialled with his right index finger, carefully holding the telephone steady. But his left hand (resting on the telephone directory, with its index finger underlining the correct number) was trembling.

"Hello?" enquired Rosa.

"Rosa?" enquired María.

"Yes, that's me. Who is it?"

Rosa sounded indifferent, formal, as if, having spoken to "the man who called her", any other voice that didn't belong to "him" would necessarily be for the Blinders, and that he – and the rest of the world – were something in which she didn't have the remotest interest.

María could sense it. He had been with Rosa on other occasions when someone rang, requesting to speak to one of the Blinders. He knew the timbre, the form, the waves of indifference her voice could transmit, all of which contrasted with the urgency which formerly only he could elicit from her. It was no longer jealousy he was experiencing but pain. The pain of exclusion.

"It's María," he said in a tone of voice which belonged to a man cast out of the world, with nothing but a coin in one hand, and a telephone in the other.

"Who?" she asked.

"It's María, Rosa. It's me. How are you? Hello? Rosa, are you there?"

"María?"

"Yes, me. What's up?"

"María?"

"Yes…"

"María, is it you?"

"Yes, yes…"

"María, good God, swear that it's really you…"

María bunched his fingertips into the form of a cross and kissed them. He was feeling emotional.

"Swear it to me," she repeated.

"I swear it."

A pause.

"María…"

"I surprised you…"

"Where have you been? Whatever happened to you?"

"Oh, well, it's just that…" he gesticulated as if to say "too long to explain".

"I can't believe it," exclaimed Rosa, and María could hear the sound of her crying.

"I'm sorry not to have called you before but…"

A sob.

"Rosa, look, things turned out in such a way that…"

Another sob.

Silence.

Then Rosa said:

"What happened?"

"It's a long story…"

"Tell me."

"I always meant to tell you… you understand me. I love you. I've never forgotten."

"Are you at home?"

"Rosa…"

"Where are you? Why are you talking in such a low voice?"

"I can't tell you that…"

"Are you well? What happened? They say you killed the foreman at your old workplace…"

"No."

"Then why do they say so? What happened to you, my darling?"

"How beautiful that you use those words to me, 'my darling'."

"They just slipped out…"

"I wish they could slip out like that all the time."

"They do slip out, but since I've heard nothing further from you…"

"You're going out with someone else?"

"No! Wherever did you get that idea from?"

"Just asking…"

"That's rubbish. I'm on my own, as before. And you? When are you going to come round? Why did you disappear like that?"

"That's what I'm about to tell you…"

"So it's all a lie, everything they say about you?"

"About killing that guy?"

"Yes…"

"Of course it is."

"Where are you, María?"

"I'm going to have to hang up, Rosa, I'm using someone else's phone…"

"Is that why you're talking so quietly?"

"Yes. And you? Are you sure there's no one else in your life?"

"You already asked me about that. The answer's still no."

"Do you think of me?"

"All the time."

"Me too."

"Wait – don't hang up!"

"How did you know I was about to hang up?"

"I know you, María. Tell me something… I don't know anything about you…"

"I've got to go."

"No, wait!"

"I'll call you back again tomorrow."

"Don't hang up!"

"Forgive me, but…"

"Wait!"

"I love you."

"María!"

"'Bye, my darling, I'll call you tomorrow. It's been wonderful talking to you," said María, and hung up.

He could feel his heart pounding throughout his body.

He waited a couple more minutes in order to regain control of himself then went downstairs to replace the telephone. Afterwards, back in his room again, he lay flat on his back on his bed and mentally reviewed everything they had said to each other. All of a sudden he heard a sound away to his right. He turned his head in the direction of the wardrobe and paused a few moments.

"I rang her," he told the rat. And he smiled.

10

The second floor was where he spent most of his time, given its wealth of available facilities. He got into the habit of sitting on the sofa completely naked, legs stretched out in front of him and ankles resting on the coffee table, reflecting on his options of getting out of the house without going to prison. He always thought in terms of "options", in the plural, even though he never got as far as encountering so much as a single one. There was nowhere for him to go. In any case, he was considerably better off here than in his own home, even assuming he'd had a home to call his own. And he no longer thought in terms like "if I were free" with bitterness, but with rejoicing: the street signified his prison sentence. Or that was how he put it to himself. On the other hand, what he missed from the outside world, though unable to approach it, was available to him there indoors. All except for one thing: cigarettes.

He had smoked a pack of twenty a day for over twenty years, and all of a sudden… The funny thing was that he did not really feel like smoking: it was the image of himself smoking, the performance of this habit, that never gave out. He had thought of leaving the "vice" behind him a thousand times, but he had never got beyond thinking of it; he was that sure of the impossibility of giving up, it was doomed from the start.

So what on earth could be the point of suffering all those symptoms of abstinence? Now, obliged not to smoke, it suddenly occurred to him that nothing had followed from his giving up: he'd suffered no particular anxieties or nervous attacks, no excessive perspiration. Neither had he experienced any particular benefit: absolutely no change had resulted in his energy levels, his senses of taste or smell, all was precisely the same as it was before. For over twenty years he had been the victim of a fictitious addiction.

How?

He took his feet off the cane coffee table, and folded his arms thoughtfully.

What had he done in his life?

His mother had gone off with another man. Almost at once, his father brought another woman home. María loathed her. So did his father, but he couldn't stand to live alone. María left. He travelled as far as Capilla del Señor and installed himself in a tiny room at the back of a house belonging to his uncle and aunt. They were very distant relatives, so he was obliged to pay rent. A symbolic amount. María picked up any old full-time job, and in the rare hours when he had nothing to do, he wandered about alone, mostly because his uncle was a homosexual and kept hitting on him. Why had he never walked out? That's where symbolism came into it: the rent was so low that María preferred to put up with the uncle. The truth of it was that years had passed without him exchanging a word with anyone, apart from insults and greetings. He couldn't recall having sustained even half a conversation with anyone in his entire life. He communicated by looks with his one and only friend. He never watched television: the TV was in the living room, with his uncle forever planted in front of it. He read. He had got himself enrolled in the library belonging to the Volunteer Fire Brigade, and took out a novel a week, selecting those with the best covers, or with the most promising titles. On the whole he proved lucky. But despite the fact he was what people generally called "a good-looking lad", nothing ever went right for him where women were concerned. He liked them only until they opened their mouths. In contrast, they liked him until they realized that he was never going to open his. He was too sullen and serious, too introverted. He found whores easier to deal with. All of them, with the exception of the kindly ones who didn't charge him to sleep with them, and who then had too much to say for themselves.

So there he was, without family, conversation, friends, love or television. What on earth, then, had he done with his life? He didn't know. But this was one question: it was only when he had asked himself a great number, all together or one after another, piling them up on top of each other, that he found the answer. Rosa.

It was the best thing that had happened to him, and it was instantaneous: a revolution at first sight. Rosa had attracted him like a magnet. He remembered that afternoon at the exit to the Disco supermarket, how as he crossed the street to their meeting, he felt himself literally drawn towards her. He crossed the street like a zombie, his mind a blank, without the least idea of what he was going to say. Fortunately it had all gone well, arguably too well: they talked briefly about Shakira and the Disco supermarket, and from that moment on, María was a new man, cheerful, chatty and confident. He no longer had to eat dirt in the way he used to.

Sometimes he'd wake in the middle of the night, not knowing where he was... He didn't know where the window was, nor the door... He'd go back to sleep only when he "understood" he was asleep. When morning rose, he'd feel dislocated all over again. The room and each one of his petty daily indicators, the handle on his little coffee pot, the direction of his shadow, the way his chair was facing, every single thing pointed towards her...

It was true: Rosa was indeed all he missed from the outside world, she alone was really essential to him. So who was the guy ringing her?

María had called her on 20th November. On that occasion he'd promised to call her back the following day, which he hadn't done. And not because he hadn't wanted to – if it were down to him, he'd have been calling her at any or every moment of the morning, noon or night – but because he had been left with the impression that Rosa had heard him "from too close at hand" and, just in case, decided not to phone again until the impression (his impression of Rosa's impression) had faded. In spite of the fact that various days of silence had followed his reappearance, it had succeeded in cooling the flirtation between Rosa and "the guy". The result of his call was obvious: Rosa preferred him to the other one. But it was also obvious that if he disappeared again, Rosa would be bound to revive the relationship with the other guy. And so it happened.

Day after day, the guy's phone calls continued with increasing frequency. By the end, he was ringing her at all hours. Sometimes Rosa would be on her own, but most of the time Señor and Señora Blinder were there too, and María found himself obliged to undertake large detours around the house in order to locate himself somewhere within earshot. From what Rosa was saying, from the cadences and oscillations in her voice, her flirtatiousness had manifestly revived.

María deduced that the guy was without pride and that, in consequence, could be a rival to be wary of, for even after Rosa had given him the cold shoulder, he had persisted to the point where the relationship could be rekindled, and so it did. On 3rd December, María called her again.

"Rosa…"

"María! Where are you? What happened?"

"Let's not go over that again, please. Are you well?"

"Yes. How about you?"

"I'm very well. A little bird told me that you're out seeing someone…"

"What little bird?"

"Little bird?"

"I don't know. You mentioned a little bird…"

"A friend, an acquaintance, if you like. I don't know whether you remember, one day when we left the hotel in the Bajo, we bumped into him and I introduced you…"

"I don't remember…"

"It doesn't matter. He told me he spotted you out the other day with someone…"

"It's a lie."

"Why would he lie to me?"

"How would I know? I don't know him... But tell him to stop telling tales, and that certainly this one isn't true."

"Are you sure?"

"María, my love, what's happened and where are you, why don't you come? I beg you: don't leave me hanging on like this. Tell me something, even if... Hello, María?"

"I'm here."

"Don't you love me any more?"

"I adore you."

"Me too."

"Me too."

"So, now?"

"Who's the guy?"

"What guy?"

"Does he work in the Disco?"

"Why are you doing this to me?"

"They told me you go out every week with one of the gardeners from the villa here. Is that him?"

"Who tells you these things, your friend? Some great friend if that's what he's filling your head with."

"Do they have a gardener, yes or no?"

"Yes, but the guy they have..."

"Is it him?"

"He who?"

"Don't you turn my words back on me, Rosa, you know full well what I'm saying to you..."

"My God..."

María was dying to be explicit. The real question was "Who keeps phoning you?" – but there was no way he could ask such a question.

"They seized you," Rosa suddenly said.

"Eh?"

"They grabbed you, you're a prisoner," said Rosa, crying. "That's why you don't want to say anything to me, because they've taken you prisoner. My darling, you have no idea what I…"

"I'm not in jail, Rosa."

"It doesn't matter…"

"I'm really not, I'm here."

"Here, where?"

"Free… here… here at large…"

"I don't believe you. I know these things, María. Doesn't matter. Tell me where you are and I'll come and see you. It doesn't matter if you're a prisoner, I swear by my children. I don't have any children, but all the same, I swear by all I hold most dear. To me, you…"

"Rosa…" said María.

And hung up.

He couldn't bear it. He was convinced that she had again managed to put her inclination to surrender to her new caller on ice, whoever he might be. What he could least bear was to hear her without seeing her, and to see her without being seen. He set down the phone and approached Rosa's room.

Rosa had just come in. María could hear her sobbing and hugged himself as if he were hugging her. He bore her in his heart, as if he had truly embraced and enfolded her.

11

One night he helped himself to a book by Dr Wayne W. Dyer entitled *Your Erroneous Zones* from the library. It was a revelation. He felt the book spoke to him (something which had never occurred with the novels, which merely kept him occupied).

Given that at least for the time being he no longer needed to concern himself with phone calls from his rival, since his own most recent call to Rosa had caused a further cooling between her and him, he devoted himself to reading. He read with a dedication and a concentration hitherto unknown to him.

It was all true. There was no phrase or idea, or statistic, or commentary, or fact, which did not resonate with a note of truth in his conscience. Every time he opened the book (something he would do only very infrequently in the course of a day, since he almost never closed it) he had a light-bulb moment. A light went on in his brain and he was dazzled. And at the same time the book left him feeling utterly stupid: he could scarcely believe he had never previously noticed that things were like that, or that they functioned in this particular manner.

The application with which he had pursued his domination of the house (so that he now knew it right down to its trivial details, including all about the bidet in one of the second-floor bathrooms, a bidet somehow designed in such a way that it was impossible to sit on the rim and dry your feet with a towel, or to engage in any other activity which failed to conform to its principal function, for fear of falling in, as though the bidet were inclined to swallow you up) was now directed towards his own internal world, where the revelations provided in the sugared pills proffered by the book affected him in a particular fashion. His desire to derive benefit from everything he read meant that his reading became tortuous. He would read phrases like: "there are men who manipulate forgetfulness with malice, much as if they were dealing punches", asking himself what to "manipulate forgetfulness with malice" actually meant, what was Doctor Dyer alluding to with "manipulate forgetfulness" and even questioning the meaning of the word "manipulate".

Using a few blank sheets of paper he had previously taken from the desk, he jotted down the most important sentences. He went back over it, rereading passages; he paused, but he also progressed. Ten days later, when he had finished the book, he felt different, enriched, vindicated.

That night he undertook his most daring action since moving into the villa: he went out of the kitchen... out into the open air... The excursion hardly lasted more than a moment, just enough to cast a glance over his surroundings. But on seeing the street (and the starless sky above) for the first time in a long while with his feet on the ground, an idea arose which doubled his daring: to exit through the barred gate, make a hurried copy of the key; return and ring the bell, embrace Rosa, make love with her, bid her farewell; all before returning indoors... He knew the house by touch, including its sounds, its movements... Nothing there at all to prevent his projected undertaking.

Back in his room again, he recounted his idea to the rat. All of a sudden, he heard the sound of a struggle on the ground floor; he was so enraptured with his daydream that it took a while to realize he was overhearing a struggle which had been initiated several minutes earlier. He ran full tilt downstairs.

Álvaro was harassing Rosa. He was pursuing her from the kitchen into the corridor, and from the corridor into the bedroom. Indignation cloaked María with invisibility: for an instant he believed himself capable of emerging from his hiding place and coming to Rosa's defence, without being seen by either of the pair of them.

12

The scene of Álvaro's harassing Rosa had replaced the miracle of *Your Erroneous Zones*. For days now he had been staring at the dust jacket of the book lying on his bed, with the sensation of never having read it. He thought of nothing and no one but Álvaro.

One morning he was cutting his hair in the bath when he heard strange noises coming from the ground floor. He took fright, knowing that both the Blinders and Rosa had only just left the house. It was one of those extremely rare occasions when nobody else was in the villa. The Blinders had gone out in a hurry, leaving an odour of perfume hanging in the air behind them; Rosa had accompanied them as far as the garage and, once the car had departed, had locked the side gate: no doubt she'd gone off on some errand or other… María heard a grunt, a muffled crash, and his freshly cut hair bristled. Who could be in the house? Hurriedly, he gathered up some curls that had fallen on the floor, wrapped them in a piece of newspaper, and secreted them in his pocket.

He descended slowly, scissors in hand. He could see Rosa from up on the first floor: she was retreating in the direction of the living room, followed by Álvaro. Whenever had they arrived? How come he never heard them enter?

Álvaro caught up with Rosa in the corridor on the way to the lounge.

"Álvaro, I beg you…" she said.

"Just a minute," Álvaro had grabbed hold of her uniform with one hand, as if he'd just captured a thief after a lengthy chase through the entire house. He was out of breath.

María descended another floor down the main staircase into the entrance hall, hiding behind a wall at the end of the corridor, barely a few yards' distance from them. He peeped around the corner and saw Álvaro grabbing Rosa. He inhaled sharply.

"Why are you trying to escape me like this?"

"Please…"

"That's quite enough of 'please'. What's up with you? Do I scare you?"

"Yes, sir."

"Call me Álvaro… it wasn't so long ago you called me Álvaro… So why are you scared of me, might I ask?"

"I don't want to…"

"You don't want to tell me?"

"No… Yes… I can tell you. But I don't want what…"

"You don't want what I want?"

Rosa nodded. Álvaro clicked his tongue, grabbed her by the belt and attempted to kiss her. Rosa threw her head back and tried to shake herself free, tugging from side to side and struggling to break loose, but Álvaro subdued her by force. He had buried his face in Rosa's neck, and was kissing it violently and spasmodically, like a vampire.

María emerged from his hiding place without thinking: Álvaro had his back to him, maybe four or five yards away. He had just taken a first step towards him, scissors raised, when suddenly Rosa succeeded in breaking loose. She turned on her heels and set off running towards the library.

María backed off.

Álvaro straightened up, and ran his fingers around the inside of his collar. He stayed there a few minutes, breathing irregularly. He seemed inclined to let her go. He took a small hip flask out of a pocket deep inside his jacket, just a quarter bottle inside a leather sleeve, took a large gulp and swallowed. He then dried his lips off with the back of his hand, stowed it away again, and paused for a moment, flicking through some papers lying on the table. Finally he set off in the direction of the library.

María followed him. The library covered a vast area, and was filled from floor to ceiling with books with dark spines. There was nowhere for Rosa to hide in there, but María entered softly calling her name, as if they were playing hide-and-seek. He slowly made his way towards the door leading into the living room, and from there continued on into the dining room.

"Rosa?" he called out.

He searched for her in the annexe to the dining room and in the study, before finally going down the service staircase. María kept one room behind him: he only entered each room as Álvaro left it. Everything was quiet. All his attention was focused on not missing his footing, on not being discovered. He couldn't afford to let himself be seen. He knew that if Álvaro spotted him, he'd have to kill him. He would have enjoyed killing him, but that would necessarily have spelled his own end. What would he do if Álvaro found Rosa and resumed the attack? It was clear that this was why Álvaro was pursuing her, but what would he – María – do if this actually happened? It was possible that Álvaro wouldn't find her: Rosa knew every nook and cranny of the house as well as he did. In any case, the best course of action for Rosa was to leave the house if she wanted to escape being raped; if she was going to be intelligent about it, she'd stay away from the villa until Señor and Señora Blinder returned.

Just then María heard the sound of a door slamming. For a moment he stood still in confusion; then he realized it had been a door on the ground floor. Had Rosa done what he knew she needed to do in order to escape Álvaro? No. It wasn't the street door that had slammed. It was the door to her bedroom. María clenched his teeth with frustration: Rosa had taken refuge in the worst possible place. And no doubt Álvaro had heard her too. María could imagine him smiling... Álvaro paused on the bottom step; he took out the bottle again, and gulped another couple of swigs. Then he went back out into the corridor.

María decided against going down the same route again: the service staircase was narrow and dark, and there was always the chance that Álvaro would also retrace his steps and make a detour to catch up again with Rosa in the kitchen, blocking her exit to the street. That would mean María would have to take him on from the front, without the least chance of hiding himself. Rather than take this risk he ran up a flight of stairs, along the length of an L-shaped passage, down again via the main staircase, to reappear at the other end of the service wing. No sign whatsoever of Álvaro.

María approached the door to Rosa's bedroom. Silence. He put his ear to the door. He couldn't hear a thing, but something told him Rosa and Álvaro must be inside. He bent down to look through the keyhole. There was no one inside.

He left and proceeded along the corridor on tiptoe, pausing at every door on the way to the top of the staircase. Disconcerted, he went on up. They didn't seem to be anywhere… Where on earth could they have gone? That was when he heard unfamiliar voices, those of a woman and children on the ground floor… The children had just come in and were running to and fro. The woman scolded them, but the kids evaded her and carried on running and shouting until a man intervened, whom Señor Blinder asked to calm down. Now it became possible to hear a child's sobbing. María, who on hearing them enter had retreated with his back to the wall, took a step forwards and caught a glimpse of a blonde woman and a young man crossing the entrance hall, dragging their suitcases behind them.

He had seen the woman in a photograph: she was the Blinders' daughter. The man had to be her husband, and the children their offspring. One of the kids must have been about fifteen. The other two – a boy and a girl – appeared considerably younger than him, maybe between six or eight years old.

Señora Blinder called for Rosa. Every second that Rosa failed to appear increased her irritation. The man deposited the suitcases at the bottom of the staircase: it was clear they had arrived to stay for a while in the house and they were going to install themselves on the first floor. That was when María heard Rosa's voice as she entered the room.

It was impossible to see out from his hidden position, but he could hear her perfectly clearly, and she sounded agitated.

"Señora Loli, what a pleasure…"

"How are you, Rosa?"

"Very well. Goodness gracious, how the children have grown. Can this really be Esteban?"

"Wherever were you?" This was Señora Blinder.

"Esteban, come here and say hello to Rosa..." called Loli.

"I was in the garden, Señora. I didn't hear you arrive..."

Señor Blinder told her:

"Be off now and prepare the guest room." She swivelled round to look at her daughter. "Do you want the kids to sleep here?" She pointed at the ground floor.

"Yes, it's probably better."

"Good afternoon, Señor Ricardo," said Rosa, greeting Loli's husband.

María couldn't hear the reply, leaving him to assume that Ricardo had responded with a shrug or a smile.

Next he heard Esteban.

"Hello, Rosa."

"My goodness, look how big you've grown..."

"It's been so long..."

"How old are you now? Fifteen?"

"Fourteen."

"So it's that long since I've seen you..." Rosa thought aloud.

"Two years," agreed Esteban.

The smallest ones also came up to greet her. They were talking in English. Neither María nor Rosa could understand a word of what they were saying. Esteban translated:

"Tony says he wants to eat veal escalopes. And Rita wants to know if you'll take them out for a treat."

There followed a silence. Rosa must have been looking at Rita's mother or father – the little girl had the same name as Señora Blinder – in search of approval, before promising yes. Esteban added:

"I've told her about your wonderful escalopes."

"Of course I'll make them for you..." said Rosa.

Just then, María heard a "hello, hello, hello", feigning a welcome. It was Álvaro.

Señor and Señora Blinder were clearly surprised to find Álvaro in the house. They said as much. Álvaro didn't bother to reply, but immediately went over to say hello once more to Loli and Ricardo. Neither they nor their children appeared in the least pleased to find him there. Loli asked him if he'd been asleep: his face looked as if it had only just left the pillow, Señor Blinder commented loudly, adding – but as if he'd really intended muttering under his breath – that he hoped he hadn't slept in his bed. It seemed Álvaro was in the habit of going to bed – drunk – in his parents' bedroom. He himself had seen him there on at least one occasion – and this was a source of annoyance to Señor Blinder.

But María knew perfectly well that Álvaro hadn't been sleeping... Why on earth had his sister told him his face looked "as if it had just left the pillow"? Álvaro began trying to tell his father that he hadn't been asleep, that really he'd been... But María couldn't overhear the remainder of his answer because Rosa had started climbing the stairs hauling up one of the suitcases, leaving him no option but to get out of the way. He was certain that Rosa had left the living room deliberately, as soon as Álvaro had entered it.

13

That was on the 21st December. Over the next three days, María learned a number of new things: that Loli and Ricardo lived in London; that neither of them were smokers (although Esteban, the fourteen-year-old, was, except he was always out of cigarettes); that the other two children spoke scarcely any Spanish and, to revert to Esteban again, that he got on extremely well with Rosa. It was on a previous visit, when Rosa had only been working in the villa for a few months, that Esteban had become such great friends with her. Esteban was only twelve at the time, with no one to open up to (in either global hemisphere), and had made Rosa his chosen confidante. It seemed he had revealed some kind of an intimate secret to her. María never discovered what it was about, but it was a closer bond even than friendship between the two of them.

"So how *are* you?" Esteban enquired of Rosa, one day when the two of them were alone in the kitchen together.

"Fine. And you?"

"Fantastic. Do you know what? What I wanted you to know," said Esteban – he was an Argentine living in London, but he'd spent most of his short life in Spain – "was that I've never stopped thinking about you for a single day."

"You?" asked Rosa, suddenly startled. "About me?"

"Of course."

"Why?"

"Don't laugh. It's true: I've thought about you every day of my life."

"You're making fun of me…"

"Come off it. Do you mean the same thing hasn't occurred to you?"

"You're talking like a screen lover! "

"That's nice of you."

"No, I'm serious! You're talking as if you were a film star…"

"If you say so…"

Silence.

A moment later, Esteban spoke out gravely:

"Naturally, I've also thought of suicide. But don't get alarmed: it wasn't you who saved me; it was I myself, because at those moments I had the good luck to think of you."

"What a poet you are…" Rosa commented.

"I've been published."

"Really?"

"No, that's a joke. But I'm writing it down. Writing all of it, every single detail of what passed between us, every least…"

"Tell me that's not true!" Rosa interrupted. Esteban bunched his fingers in the sign of the cross, and kissed them.

Rosa grew indignant:

"You'll get me thrown out!"

"I'll make you famous."

Silence.

"It is a joke, isn't it?"

"You tell me if you remembered me, and I'll tell you whether or not it's a joke."

Silence.

"Yes, you know it's true," Rosa finally said. "Now tell me yourself: is it a joke?"

"Would you believe me if I told you it was?"

Silence.

Followed by giggles.

María couldn't see nor hear him, but in his head he visualized Esteban and Rosa emerging from a long embrace. A second later and the two of them were laughing and chatting at high speed, without either accusations or histrionics.

María was overcome with fascination. What had taken place between the pair of them? The serenity and self-confidence demonstrated by Esteban had made him think (more than was suggested by what he was saying) that he was dealing with a lad too clever for his years. Soon he'd also be thinking that within the panorama of his true intentions towards Rosa, friendship didn't feature much larger than a peanut. Jealousy was to come later. For the time being, he was extremely busy processing fresh information.

For a start, cohabitation (as María called it, despite never having been invited in) had become extremely difficult. Since there were now so many more occupants in the house, basic and essential acts, such as going to the toilet or the kitchen, demanded an exhausting degree of attentiveness. And he couldn't even sleep well, for fear that one or another of the little kids would decide to conduct an exploration of the house. The house scared and tempted them in equal measures. Even the rat seemed stressed out. Lack of sleep, irregular eating habits, a constant state of alertness... it was too much. Every hour seemed like a century. And it already appeared they were going to stay into the new year! And to cap it all – and this was worst of it – he still hadn't managed to find out what had taken place between Álvaro and Rosa.

He didn't learn until the afternoon of the 24th December. Meanwhile he had brought a few happy actions to a successful conclusion that would be useful in the future (since to enjoy them now meant absenting himself from what appeared truly important to him): he'd robbed Esteban of the headphones to his Walkman, and he'd even managed to steal one of the bottles of champagne reserved for parties from the kitchen. It was a long time since he'd drunk alcohol, and he couldn't remember ever having tasted champagne. That afternoon, on the 24th, the

Blinders and their guests had gone out en masse to buy Christmas presents, leaving María to take it easy, at least for a few hours, a rare opportunity to be near Rosa. He watched her ironing, changing the sheets, cooking, nibbling at bits of food, bending her fingers backwards – since the Blinders' relations had come to stay, she no longer masturbated – and finally dial a telephone number.

"He raped me."

"..."

"Rosa."

"..."

"He raped me."

"..."

"Álvaro."

"..."

"Yes."

"..."

"Yes, he raped me. What do you mean, *how* did he rape me? He raped me!"

"..."

"I knew that…"

"..."

"Nothing, I defended myself, but I don't know how, he grabbed me and…"

"..."

"No, thank God. At least not that. He just gagged my mouth… He's big and strong and he was drunk. There wasn't exactly much I could do…"

"..."

"You. Only you."

"..."

"Come on, what kind of an accusation can I make, with the money they have. Also…"

"…"

"No, I won't do that."

"…"

"It's like…"

"…"

"No!"

"…"

"Oh he's been after me for quite a while and you know, I…"

"…"

"Are you crazy? How can I possibly tell them something like this? If I tell them, they'll throw me out!"

"…"

"So then where would I go?"

"…"

"Listen, Claudia, I tell you the guy came in and raped me and the only bit that matters to you is legal action? What happened to me doesn't count?"

"…"

"And so what?"

María's hands were shaking. That bastard Álvaro had raped Rosa! He longed to cry, but he was so furious he suppressed his rage. Rage likewise forestalled him from listening to the rest of the conversation. Rosa hung up and as she did so, the phone began ringing. Rosa answered.

"Hello?" she said. Her voice still held a tremor from the previous conversation.

The person on the other end clearly observed this.

"Nothing, nothing," replied Rosa.

"…"

"No, honestly, it's nothing."

"…"

"No, everything's fine."

106

"…"

"Well, just hanging out here…"

"…"

"Yes, I also wondered about that…"

"…"

"When?"

"…"

"I don't know, all these relatives have arrived and it looks like I'll be running around like crazy…"

"…"

"Like a loose canon, yes."

"…"

"And as for you, how are you?"

"…"

"God, but it's true what I'm telling you. I won't say definitely no, but… Another day, perhaps…"

It was "the guy". María had suspected as much, but now, with that "another day, perhaps", he had proof. Rosa had held him on standby as a result of his latest phone call, but at the same time wasn't going to give him a definitive no, meaning that the caller wasn't just anyone, but "the guy". She liked him, life was giving her a "second chance" and, just in case – since María was still the first one, even if he was appearing out of it – he was still being allowed a little space.

"The only thing missing now," thought María, "is that she tells him she got raped and we'll have the whole bloody love story." He said this to himself suddenly, without aforethought, lucidly, without feeling himself feeling it, without resentment and without laughing out loud. And then he heard her say:

"One little problem…"

"…"

"Here, it's private."

María saw what was coming and feared the worst. Was Rosa really so desperate to tell everyone else that she'd been raped? He felt disgusted by rapists; he had no other views on them, or feelings towards them; they just revolted him. But he didn't understand that the victim, and Rosa more than all the rest, was unable to overcome her indignation, and, in her anxiety for protection, felt obliged to bring it out into the open, instead of keeping quiet and conserving energies better deployed in revenge. To him, this was the essential difference between a man and a woman. The woman *relates* what she intends to do, and prays for someone else to do it.

María thought Rosa was very intelligent, but didn't think she had too much competence in dealing with this matter: he wanted to be the one to get to Álvaro. This was why her way of unburdening herself to everyone else bothered him, because in the telling she fabricated a rival and, at the same time, left him at a disadvantage: it left María with far fewer options for his kind of rough justice. The guy was out on the street and could be intercepted either head on, or by feigning a casual accident, and then beaten to death. Only not by him. He was obliged to wait. On the other hand, he loathed to overhear Rosa discuss sex with anyone else.

Who was the guy? What could he do to check him out? It was a good moment to call her (he was on his own). He went upstairs to look for the portable phone and dialled the number of the house. Busy. This was surprising because Rosa had hung up. He called again. Engaged. Had the guy called? Or had Rosa called him? Perhaps she was just taking an anodyne call from someone…

While he was waiting for Rosa to finish speaking, he occupied himself by going through the possessions of

Loli and Ricardo. There was nothing there to catch his attention: passports and clothes and more clothes... In the bedside table drawer he found a penknife: he kept it. In a folder marked "American Airlines" he discovered a wad of notes. He counted them: they totalled $4,500.

He weighed the folder in his hand, as if it were a brick. He would have had to slave for years to earn money like this; what was curious was how little the labour of so many years weighed. What would he do, keep it? How would the Blinders react, would they think a thief had entered in their absence or would they fall to blaming one another? He couldn't take the risk: it was more than likely they'd blame Rosa. They'd chuck her out. And what about him? Could he go on living in the villa without Rosa? Or would he have no alternative but to leave? No, he was incapable of remaining a single day longer in the house without Rosa. And at the same time, he would have to remain there, otherwise when they threw her out and he followed, he'd end up in jail as soon as they caught him, so that way he wouldn't see her again either. Prison had to be a far worse place than the villa, of this there could be no doubt.

The dollars enraged him. He had never as much as held a dollar in his hand, and now that he was holding four thousand five hundred, they were useless to him. He resumed dialling the phone number. It remained engaged. He went to take a look at what was going on.

He went downstairs, annoyed with Rosa, treading on the flat of his foot, as if sending a message to once and for all kindly hang up the phone. But Rosa wasn't in the kitchen. María was scared: he had been certain of finding her there – and had allowed himself to be led by his assumption that the engaged tone necessarily signalled that the line was in use... He had been so certain that when he didn't find her there, he suddenly became concerned that she might just make him jump by turning up behind his back.

His eyes took in the kitchen at a glance, as if they were a camera lens, so he beat a rapid retreat, mentally going over the details of what he had seen and now imprinted on his mind as he saw them: bottles of champagne, piles of table napkins on the sideboard, a lit stove (Rosa might return at any moment) and the telephone half-hanging off its hook.

"Pheew!" he exhaled.

For an instant (mid-air as he left by silent leaps and bounds) he contemplated the possibility of returning to replace the handset correctly. The burning stove meant that Rosa couldn't be too far from the kitchen, even though, thinking it through carefully, a stove is one of those artefacts that afford the cook time (the other side of the coin to, say, a liquidizer). Impossible to guess where Rosa might be at this juncture... Yet just in case, he hesitated. Whatever happened, he decided to stay put: he wanted to know just as soon as possible what Rosa's reaction would be to finding the telephone off the hook. He had to speak to her today, come what may.

He went into one of the ground-floor toilets. He was naked and sat down at once on the lavatory seat. He stayed there, with the bored expression of someone waiting for someone else in order to complete a piece of business, but after a few minutes, he stretched out one leg, shunted the door with his foot, half-closing it, and began to strain at his labours.

He remembered that when he was a kid, he'd always been a leader. And he realized that never, right up until now, had he understood why. He had been a quiet child and mysterious along with it. That was all. He had no other virtues. At that time he'd not had a quarter of the agility he now possessed. But his friends and acquaintances respected and feared him.

It's always a problem to talk when you really have something to say. But having it all without saying a thing is magical, and you need to be a magician to enjoy the role. María was the opposite: he found himself out of sorts and uncomfortable. He knew that without a doubt he was going to be discovered and ejected, rubbished. He was a false leader. He had been a false acolyte. Would he also be?… Be careful: someone had just come in.

María emerged from the toilet and, for a fraction of a second, he found himself face to face with Señora Blinder. She didn't actually see him, but when he backed off and hid inside a bedroom, he was left with an overall image of exactly what Señora Blinder was wearing, right down to the gems in her necklace.

He hid behind the door. Señora Blinder entered, switched on the light, lifted the cover on the ottoman at the foot of the bed, removed something from inside, and left the room again. A few seconds later she reappeared. This time she seated herself on the bed, rested the palms of her hands on her thighs, and looked left and right without any apparent reason: she didn't crane her neck, she wasn't looking for anything… Then she got up, went to the window, examined the curtains, shook them as if to air them, then went over and sat at a desk, where she remained without moving for several minutes. María thought that people who are watched without knowing it appear mad.

Until Señor Blinder came in and everything became normal again.

Señor Blinder walked to and fro, clearly longing to launch an insult (but restraining himself like a gentleman), while Señora Blinder slowly turned her face to look at him.

"Something up?" she asked him.

"And you're asking me..." he replied.

She blinked. She recognized his tone as a battle cry and, even while she didn't yet understand what he was referring to by his "and *you're* asking *me*", accepted the rebuke.

"Are you annoyed?" she enquired.

Señor Blinder stopped and stared at her.

"Of course I'm annoyed," he said.

"What are you talking about?" Señora Blinder asked, with genuine sincerity.

"The toilet," he said.

"What's up with the toilet?"

"And you're asking me?"

Señora Blinder paused once more. She looked sideways, then let her eyes slide back to look at him again:

"What sort of nonsense is this?" she said. "I'm asking you what's going on in the toilet. What *is* going on?"

"Go and see for yourself if you want," said Señor Blinder, his tone sounding both ironic and fed up.

Señora Blinder didn't move. The only thing she did was to take her eyes off her husband and fix them on a spot on the wall, thinking deeply. Then she rose and left the bedroom.

When she returned, she looked as if she'd witnessed a crime.

"Do you think I did that!" she said.

"Why not? Did I do it?" Señora Blinder replied sarcastically.

Señora Blinder clenched her fists.

"Have you gone mad?" she asked.

"Go on, Rita, pull the chain and let's go to sleep, it's getting late," he said, and sat down on the bed and pulled off his shoes.

Señora Blinder took three steps towards her husband.

"In the first place, it wasn't me. Secondly, let's not hear anything about 'let's get to bed': it's seven-thirty in the evening, and we have guests. You're going to take a shower, and we'll all have dinner together. Where on earth did you get the idea that I could have left a thing that size in the toilet?"

"Rita, until this point in our conversation, I was merely joking. But if you carry on like this, you'll end up really infuriating me. Pull the chain and let's change the subject."

"I tell you, it wasn't me!"

"OK, it was me. Can you please now go and pull the chain?"

"No!" replied Señora Blinder, and crossed her arms.

"Why are you shouting?" asked Señor Blinder, wrinkling his nose in disgust, as if his wife's voice was unbearable to him.

"Marcos, if you're annoyed about what happened today with Ricardo, don't take it out on me, it's not fair. Even less when you pick a fight about something like *this*," went on Señora Blinder, waving in the direction of the toilet. "We're grown-ups."

"I don't want an argument..."

"I do! By this stage I absolutely do need an argument!"

"Then have it with yourself. If you want to argue with me, first go and pull the chain. I want to take a shower."

"Unbelievable."

"My opinion entirely."

"What's your problem with Ricardo, what's up with you? He's your daughter's husband! He's been married to her for nine years, he hasn't just parachuted in from the skies above. You know him. You know what he's like. The other fellow... well, all right he really was an idiot."

"But he's the children's father..."

"Only of one of them!"

"The best one of them..." Señor Blinder said in a low voice.

"You're so unfair," his wife reproached him. "Those children are also your grandchildren."

"I've nothing at all to say about them! What does bother me is seeing how they put that lad down. It annoys me. What do you want me to do? Esteban loves him, he's his father and needs to see him... he has the right to see him..."

"He's a drug addict."

"That's a lie!" announced Señor Blinder. "They want to get rid of him. Hans would never touch drugs!"

"Come off it, Marcos... he was put in prison, in Holland too. You know perfectly well that you have to be in possession of a pretty large quantity to get put inside in a country like Holland, don't you, eh?"

"They framed him."

"That's his story..."

"And I believe it. It's political. Politics is the same the whole world over."

Señora Blinder made a suggestive pause.

"They released him. They must have their reasons," went on Señor Blinder. Under the Argentine military dictatorships he had endlessly reiterated his ideas based on no more than "they must have their reasons"; now the country was a democracy, he was saying "they must have their reasons". Denial of personal responsibility as superior mental entelechy.

Señora Blinder had lost her appetite for an argument. She marched out of the bedroom and did not return, but Señor Blinder and María heard her pull the chain. María was convinced that Señora Blinder had given in to her husband through a process of attrition, while deeming it impossible to deal with a man like him. He was also certain that Señor Blinder loathed her, even if not quite as much as she detested him.

14

When Álvaro arrived, María was hidden in the kitchen annexe, observing a conversation taking place between Esteban and Rosa. It was eleven o'clock at night. The Blinders had finished their dinner and were taking their coffee in the living room, while the younger children were playing Tetris on a laptop.

Esteban had installed himself in the kitchen. Every time Rosa returned from the dining room (she went to and fro bringing back dirty plates and setting the table for the midnight toast), Esteban exchanged a few words with her.

María monitored the two situations at first hand, slipping from the kitchen annexe (where he could overhear without watching the exchanges between Esteban and Rosa), to the first floor (from where he could both watch and hear – at least in part – the scene involving the Blinders). He recognized a degree of complicity between Esteban and Rosa, in consequence of something that must have occurred quite a while back when

Esteban was only ten or twelve years old; the issue was that now the lad was rather more grown up, he seemed set on converting complicity into union. And Rosa was leading him on, laughing under her breath and agreeing with whatever he said.

Despite his jealousy, María stayed watching the scene being played out by the Blinders. Álvaro absorbed all his attention. He despised him. Álvaro was unusually – miraculously – sober, and to begin with, María found it hard to single him out: his voice sounded like someone else's.

The first thing Álvaro did was to serve himself a brandy.

"Have you eaten?" enquired his mother.

"Like a pig," replied Álvaro.

He explained he'd been to dinner at the house of a group of Alcoholics Anonymous members, and laughed as he related how they'd chased him around the table in order to gain access to his hip flask. They'd got hold of it. It now seemed, however, as if he was overcoming this setback with a vengeance: inside of ten minutes he'd downed two glasses of brandy. Protests from his mother and sister ensued, then faded to silence between the first and second glasses. They knew him, and there was nothing to be done.

Half an hour later Álvaro had regained his customary tone of voice, discussing English football in short sentences, emphasizing the word *hooligan*, which didn't bother Ricardo, but did bother his father. Señor Blinder just sat there, his mouth open and his gaze fixed on an indeterminate point between his wife and daughter, who were leafing through a photo album.

It was midnight. Christmas Day. Everyone rose and filed into the dining room. Álvaro wobbled over to the table in a series of zigzags; Ricardo uncorked a bottle of champagne while his wife shook their daughter, who had fallen asleep. Esteban reappeared just a minute before midnight, following Rosa, bearing a tray with the glasses on it. Señora Blinder invited them to clink glasses with her; afterwards they were free to do as they liked.

"I told Claudia I'd come round to celebrate a bit at her place…" said Rosa.

"If you want, you can phone and wish your mother a merry Christmas…" offered Señor Blinder.

"Thank you very much, Señor. I'll ring her in a moment."

María took the opportunity offered by the toast to go to the kitchen and help himself to dinner. Tonight he was generous to himself: he took several pasties, a large slice of roast meat, potatoes, ham, bread and a banana. He'd eaten nothing for the entire day. As he was about to withdraw he spotted a couple of empty wine bottles on the sideboard, sitting next to a half-dozen unopened bottles. Would Rosa notice if one went missing? Most likely she wouldn't; he took a bottle and set off for the attic. He carried the bottle in his left hand; in his right he bore the plate with everything else on it, including a knife and fork.

Once in his room, he levered the cork out of the bottleneck with the knife, took a small sip of wine from the bottle, swilled it around his mouth, and swallowed it.

"Merry Christmas," he told the rat, and took a larger swig.

Next he settled himself down to eat. His plate held a heap of muddled food: the ham beneath the roast, with a pasty in the middle, the potatoes on top of the banana, altogether the result of too much hurry. He

117

picked up the piece of ham and raised it to his lips. It was difficult to swallow. He was hungry, but Álvaro's presence effectively shut down his windpipe. In so far as he had managed to retain Álvaro in his line of vision, he hadn't taken his eyes off him for a second; he'd stared at him from the shadows with such fixation, it seemed extraordinary that Álvaro hadn't noticed him.

He set the plate down to one side and pushed himself back on the bed with his heels, so that his back was shoved up against the wall. He felt nauseous. An electric shiver which ran downwards from his shoulders and another which rose from his waist met in the pit of his stomach, as if that were where his rage and his relaxation had chosen to clash. He half-closed his eyes.

Then he heard a car horn, the voices of kids on the street, and felt his eyes must have closed in sleep a long, long time ago. He was confused. The rage he'd experienced towards the foreman that distant afternoon was as nothing compared with what he now felt towards Álvaro, and he wondered how he could have fallen asleep. He recalled having put a scrap of ham under the wardrobe for the rat... He had barely drunk a few sips of wine... He shook his head, and rapidly descended to the first floor.

He had no idea of the time, but it had to be late: there was no one in the dining room, and the lights were turned off on the ground floor. He ran towards Rosa's room. He didn't dare open her door, but either heard – or believed he heard – her breathing, and knew she was asleep in there.

The night had closed in; not a ray of light infiltrated from outside. María felt his way across the room from memory, reaching the Blinders' bedroom, and half-saw two motionless mounds in the bed, each completely separated from the other.

The kitchen clock showed twenty past three in the morning. He returned to the living room. He was tired, as if the hours he'd spent asleep had worn him out. He collapsed into an armchair.

On Álvaro's last visit, María had overheard him saying that it was now six months since he'd had a cigarette. Yet there was definitely the smell of nicotine in the air. He leaned slowly forwards and felt around several butts in an ashtray on the rattan table. All had been smoked down to the filter except one. He picked it up and, rolling it between his fingers like a blind man, noted there was still an inch or two of cigarette left, and that it hadn't been stubbed but left to burn out: the paper was smooth, without rips in it. He lifted it to his lips.

He didn't think of smoking it there. He put it between his lips intending to feel its shape, but what he felt was more nausea: the filter was still wet with Álvaro's saliva. He let it drop, curling his fingers in disgust, anxious only to cease physical contact with it.

Suddenly he was aware of heavy breathing, almost snoring. He got up, then froze to the spot. A man was asleep in the armchair opposite him. He was at least five yards away, across the rattan table, all of a heap, his head lolling to the left. On the back of the chair, somewhat to the right of his head, his coat was dangling; one of the coat sleeves rested on his leg.

María hauled himself up an inch at a time, and went over to the armchair; the minute hand on the kitchen clock moved faster than he did.

It was Álvaro. María controlled his own breathing. Since the man was so undeniably Álvaro, he was on the point of leaving, but decided to give him another chance: he leaned forwards and put his hands to his throat. Álvaro shrugged his shoulders as if some minor nuisance – a fly, a draught – were bothering him.

María applied more pressure. Then Álvaro opened his eyes and saw a totally nude stranger with his hands around his neck. The mixture of sleep, alcohol and the oddity of the situation raised a vague smile. He attempted to stand, but María knelt on his legs, immobilizing him, and increased the pressure on his throat.

"Hello," he said.

He pressed so hard he could hear the sound of small bones breaking.

His attention was caught by Álvaro's docility, his utter lack of resistance, as if he were in a deathly trance, while preferring to believe he were only in a dream. A few moments later, Álvaro closed his eyes and his face disappeared. María assumed his face had turned so black that it had faded into the darkness. Then he suddenly released the pressure.

He was sweating. A bead of perspiration dropped from the end of his nose; his hands and his arms were trembling. Now that he had killed Álvaro, he loathed him even more.

He remained some time kneeling on Álvaro's legs, reproaching himself for having lacked the presence of mind to tell him that the man in the process of killing him was Rosa's boyfriend. Finally, he got up and went to sit down on the sofa. He was exhausted.

"Right," he told himself, "what next?" He could open the kitchen door and take the keys, so the Blinders would assume the murderer had entered the house from outside, at some unknown hour of the night... perhaps seeking Ricardo's dollars, or Señora Blinder's jewels... He rejected the idea immediately: it was too risky to go into Ricardo's bedroom and steal the dollars, and the same applied to Señora Blinder's jewels. He lacked enough information on Álvaro's relationships with his family, or even outside of it, to try and fabricate the scenario for a crime of passion. In any case nobody would believe for more than a minute that Ricardo or Señor Blinder would be capable of murdering him: neither man had sufficient strength to strangle Álvaro, no matter how drunk he was. No one had the least suspicion as to his own presence inside the house either, so no one would be looking for him. In all likelihood, the police would convince themselves of either the one or the other of the two options he had already come up with, whether he left the doors open or not. Whichever it was, they would go over the house with a fine toothcomb, and they might even set up a base there, which would mean him expiring of thirst or hunger if he weren't discovered beforehand. The Blinders might even decide to decamp to a hotel, or to stay with friends, revolted or terrified by the murder. Then what would become of him... or of Rosa?

All this flashed through his mind in the space of a sigh. In fact, from the time he collapsed onto the sofa till the point when he got moving again, some five or six minutes had elapsed. He'd done no more than recover his breath and his strength: now he knew what he was going to do, he had no need of further thought. He had had an idea and, to judge from the speed with which he wiped the sweat from his body, it was a work of genius.

He went upstairs to his room.

On hearing him arrive, the rat jumped off the bed and lazily, confidently, headed for the cupboard. María picked up the plate of food he'd left on the bed a few hours earlier and left the room again.

He still had enough nerve to make a detour to the kitchen to check the time on the wall clock. He had been under the impression that day was dawning, but it was five in the morning. The sky had cleared, admitting a fraction more light, that was all. He had plenty of time before day broke. Nonetheless, he was worried by the difference between his perception of time and reality; he could have sworn that no more than a few minutes had gone by.

He set down the plate on the rattan table. Next he picked up Álvaro's body, dragging it from the armchair and depositing it face upwards on the sofa. He had often heard comments on the media about the deadweight of a corpse, but Álvaro's body could not have felt lighter to his touch. He sat down beside him and took a piece of meat from the plate and put it into his own mouth. He chewed it. Then he spat the masticated meat into his hand, pushed it into Álvaro's mouth, and used two fingers to force it into the bottom of his throat.

He repeated the operation until no more meat remained on the plate. Then he added the pasty, a small quantity of ham and the bread.

He had stuffed him like a turkey.

It only remained for him to hope that, if the following day there were any doubts as to the cause of Álvaro's death (asphyxia through regurgitation, or choking on his own vomit) and someone decided to visit the Alcoholics Anonymous group with whom he'd dined on Christmas Eve, this menu would fit the bill.

Apart from that – and it was fortunate that this was the case – María had lost all remnants of hunger. In fact, he felt fully satisfied. He got up, picked up the plate (nodding with approval to observe that at least the banana was still left for him) and disappeared into the darkness.

15

The first thing he did when he woke next day was to breakfast on the banana. Then he ran his tongue over the plate to lick up the remains of the meat and a plum-flavoured sauce, while conducting one of his imaginary conversations with Rosa.

"To please other people, there's no need to be beautiful but to be horrible."

"Why?"

"What do you mean, 'why'? Think about it a minute. You have to say what others want to hear, you have to smile at everyone you meet, you need to be impersonal, transparent and a whole heap of other things too, all horrible. And all to what end? In the end you die. We all die. Have you never thought that when you die, and all those you know die, nothing will be left of you, not even a memory?"

"You're being very profound..."

"No, nothing profound about it, it's a cliché. What happens is that people don't want to see it. Some because they can't and others because they see it but... What took place between you and that fellow?"

He was about to reply in Rosa's voice when *he heard it* for real:

"María!"

His breath was cut short.

He cautiously left the room, confirming that nobody else was in sight, and slipped as rapidly as possible downstairs towards the kitchen. On his way down he heard Rosa's voice again, repeatedly calling his name, now from the little garden adjoining the tradesman's entrance.

There was no one in the kitchen. The outside door was open a crack. María went over to the window and looked outside. The street entrance with its grille was also open, but Rosa was not to be seen anywhere.

A minute later, Rosa came in from the street. She was agitated, as though she'd been running. She shut and locked the street gate and walked back indoors: she looked grief-stricken. María saw her coming and hid himself behind the wall by the kitchen annexe. It wasn't a very safe place, for if Rosa decided to go and fetch something from the dining room, he'd have no escape route onto the corridor or the staircase without being seen. But Rosa sat down at the table, laid her head on her folded arms, and started to cry.

María watched her for a few moments. Then he retreated slowly towards the staircase, and ran upstairs rapidly to find the telephone. He had a million questions to ask her.

"Rosa?" he said as soon as she picked up.

"I saw you, I called you, and you behaved as if you couldn't hear me!" said Rosa all of a rush, her voice breaking. "Why do you do this to me, what happened to you, what made you change like this? Why are you playing games with me?"

María comprehended she must have caught sight of someone resembling him outside on the pavement. She had called him, run after him for a few yards – perhaps as far as the corner, but not much further, taking into account that she had left the house open and empty – shouting after him without getting an answer.

"It wasn't me you saw."

"You behaved like you were distracted, you saw me calling you but pretended you couldn't hear me!"

"It wasn't me, Rosa. You confused me with someone else."

(Sobs.)

"Tell me, how am I dressed?" asked María. At that moment, he was wearing nothing except his shirt (he had cleaned himself up a bit that morning).

"All in blue."

"See? I'm not wearing anything blue."

"And how am I supposed to know if you're lying or not, when I can't see you?"

María thought for a second.

He was on the point of saying something like "just believe me" or "why would I lie to you?" when Rosa asked him another question:

"Where are you speaking from?"

"From a public phone box…"

"Why don't you come here? Why do you never give me an explanation for what happened?"

"I love you. That's the only thing which matters."

"I love you too, and that's why I want to see you. I swear, you're doing my head in, María… I don't know why… I don't understand any of it…"

"And?"

"And what?"

"Is the other guy still pursuing you?"

"What other guy?"

"Come on Rosa, let's not start that again… Who is he?"

"It doesn't matter to you."

"You see? See, I'm right, there is another guy. Who is he?"

"No one."

"Tell me who he is."

"First you tell me what has happened, why you're behaving like this, and I'll... In any case, it doesn't matter that you go on endlessly about the big guy when I still don't know why you left like you did. I thought you loved me..."

"So he's big, is he?"

"I don't rightly know about big. He's tall."

"Do I know him?"

"I'm going to hang up. You're hassling me."

"No – wait, Rosa, this is important! I love you too..."

"I don't believe you."

"I swear to God I do. Do I know him?"

"Who?"

"Big boy, tall guy, whatever!"

Silence.

"Listen to me, Rosa. I can't tell you too much. You have to trust me, and you have to believe me. I love you and that's the truth. It's true that I love you. I'd give my right hand – and half the other one – for a kiss from you, but I can't. Listen to me carefully, my love: I can't. *I can't.* You have to be patient, because at any moment it might be possible and... well, for now, that's just the way things are."

"Are you in prison?"

"I've already told you I'm not."

"So, what?"

"Who's the big guy you've been talking about? Do I know him?"

Silence.

"Rosa?"

"I can't believe you going on endlessly about this. He's totally unimportant to me. He pursues me, but I don't even give him the time of day. The only thing I

126

do is think of you. I feel so lonely! Even more so now...
Do you remember me talking to you about Álvaro, the
Blinders' son, who drank like a fish? Well, this morning
they found him dead in the living room."

"What happened to him?"

"In my opinion, they killed him."

"What?" asked María, after a pause.

"He choked on his vomit while asleep, so they said.
He's just been buried, they didn't want to give him a
wake or anything: straight into the ground. Bah – they'd
said right in front of me, they'd give him a decent wake...
I don't know where... but it seemed to me they couldn't
wait to bury him. Nobody around here liked him."

"Why do you say he was killed?"

"I don't know... I'm afraid."

"Who would kill him here inside the house?"

"I don't know. But don't pay any attention to me. Who
knows, perhaps it's more likely he really did choke and
here's me saying otherwise, that he... My love?"

"Yes."

"Are you far away?"

"No..."

"Do you sometimes come as far as here? Oh, I need to
hang up!" said Rosa hurriedly. "Someone's coming. Call
me later. And don't worry, I've never told anyone you've
rung me... I've got to go. I love you."

And she hung up.

Almost directly afterwards Esteban came into the
kitchen. He was dressed as if for church, in a blue jacket,
grey trousers, white shirt, with a tie and soft shoes to
match.

"Watch out," he told Rosa, "Grandfather is furious: he
keeps on getting the engaged signal, all the time. And
on top of that, the other line is *also* always occupied."

"Oh my God, I must have knocked it half off the hook... when I cleaned..."

Rosa went running up to the first floor. María, who'd caught the first part of the conversation, ran on ahead of her. He had several yards advantage over her, so could reach the phone before she did. He took it off the hook and, without thinking about what he was doing, hid it behind some curtains. But Rosa was so worried by the talking-to that Señor Blinder would give her when he arrived, she didn't notice the curtains still swinging.

She reconnected the phone and made the sign of the cross. Then she looked at the phone again. It was still warm.

16

There had been no remorse, but at the same time no relief. Quite the opposite: he was worried. He would have liked to talk to Rosa, to explain to her that he was the murderer, and that he'd done it for her. He hardly expected Rosa to pat him on the back, but he longed to see her face (even with an expression of shock on it), followed by a relief which he could not feel. It was an irrational fantasy rather than a hallucination, the product of his fantastical situation: deprived as he was of speech, of being seen, even of making a noise, his fantasies swept all before them. Were he not living hidden away in the villa, but had still murdered Álvaro, it would never have crossed his mind to admit that he did it. And now on top of it all, he would have to take care when he spoke to her on the phone: it simply hadn't occurred to him that someone would want to use the spare line if the main one was constantly engaged.

For the time being, there was little to be done. For the two or three days after their return from the cemetery, the Blinders suspended their city walks and imposed a limit on the number of times they left the house. Had Señor Blinder scolded Rosa for blocking the first telephone line, and for leaving the second one disconnected? Probably not, although it was hard to be sure, given that the near-constant presence of the Blinders in their villa obliged him to stay away from the ground floor and even, at certain times, to keep off the first floor, where the Blinders had agreed to let the youngest kids have full rein to play – mostly, it seemed, at hide-and-seek.

In any case, he conducted a couple of reccies at various hours of the day, and could detect no sign whatever of grief among the Blinders. Instead of affecting them, Álvaro's death seemed to have brought them together: they went around in a band, always more than one at a time, as though the space had drawn them in. Until some kind of spontaneous and sudden accord returned them to their normal routines – and as if the period of mourning were a formality with which they were obliged to comply – the thing they did most was to spend hour after hour seated in the living-room armchairs staring at the television set, seemingly both absent and pensive. Nobody spoke, apart from the children.

That meant two long and very tedious days. He was prevented from reading by his anxiety... Why had Rosa said that she believed they'd killed Álvaro? He did his gymnastic exercises... Who was the big guy who called her up on the phone? He'd discovered that the Walkman couldn't be made to work... He was overwhelmed with an impulse to smash it on the floor, but he put it down on the bed and got up.

He pulled one slat of the venetian blinds down a couple of inches, applied an eye to the gap and took a look outside. That calmed him down. Every time he looked out, he was surprised to find that within this scrap of reality, as he called the outside world, he could see all of reality. A panorama of no more than thirty yards across, from the building with its yellow acrylic balconies to the corner on the opposite side of the street, was enough to give him a sense of the general mood, at least that of the upper classes; do the same with the unemployed, in accordance with the growth or decline in the number of cardboard collectors and street traders; learn about the latest developments in the car industry; get up to speed with news of the fashion world; know the time and the temperature and even to know all about whatever was happening on the ground floor – who came in, who went out, if another delivery of Disco shopping had arrived… At night, in the windows of cars parked in front of the house, he could see the reflections of the kitchen lights. The temperature inside the house was always lower than on the street, but an approximation of the "real" temperature was provided by the way in which people were dressed, and to gauge the time you only had to follow the haste they were making and the attitudes they assumed. Occasionally, he caught sight of Rosa: she was crossing the kitchen garden and heading towards the gate giving onto the outside street.

He liked to see her. He could feel her come alive: her face became illuminated as if she had just swallowed an air bubble, like an infant. But there was something wrong with the way Rosa looked now… She was walking slowly and pensively, with her arms folded…

That's the right word: pensively. Rosa leaned her forehead on the bars, and scarcely moved her head to left and right to look out onto the pavement. She didn't seem to be waiting for someone, rather to be looking for them. Possibly, bearing in mind her pensiveness, perhaps all this was María's own fancy. Rosa herself had shrugged her shoulders. A gentle, constant breeze was wafting her apron, without lifting it. It had to be six or seven o'clock in the evening: the shining gold of the evening made her hair look blacker than ever.

And then, out of the blue, Rosa spun round and stared upwards, towards the window. María had no time at all in which to take a step back. He stood there, paralysed, his mind working at the speed of light. If he moved away from the window, Rosa would notice the movement, and he'd be discovered.

For the space of a few seconds, which to María seemed like hours, Rosa kept her eyes glued to the gap between the slats on his venetian blind. Had she seen him and was she watching him? From her expression, he gathered that she was not: she stayed where she was, with her arms crossed. Her face showed not the faintest flicker of surprise. Surely, he thought, she wouldn't be able to see him in the darkness of the room, and instead was reproaching herself over a window she hadn't properly shut. Nonetheless, Rosa's look was directed at his eye… Not above nor below his eye, but directly at it.

Rosa ran her tongue over her lips, let her arms fall to her sides, as if she'd just noticed something dreadful, and ran into the house at full speed.

María cast a glance about the room: no change there, everything looked exactly the same as it did on the first day he entered it. He grabbed the Walkman, the headset and Dr Dyer's book. Then he left the room again, closing the door after him, and ran to hide himself in the loft.

Rosa reached the attic a minute after him. She had run upstairs and was out of breath and agitated. She went straight to María's room. But the same impetus which had brought her thus far did not carry her over the threshold: she took the final yards leading up to the door with faltering steps (indoors, up until now, no gentle breezes blew, yet her apron remained stuck to her body), as if she wanted to stop but was unable to.

She rested one hand on the handle and opened the door exceedingly slowly. She paused. For a moment it looked as if she was sniffing the air in the room, doing no more than craning her neck to peer inside. Then, still standing on the landing outside, she looked behind her, as if she knew someone were watching her from that side. Finally, she entered.

She went over to the window, one step at a time, looking to left and right, and up and down, until eventually she closed the venetian blind. María noted a rush of urgency – a rush without fear, a rush of relief, a return to normality. "*It was nothing.*" She was on the point of leaving when, all of a sudden, something made her scream. She let out such a piercing shriek that it was heard all the way down to the ground floor.

Señor Blinder's voice reached the attic with only a few seconds' delay:

"Something up?"

Rosa emerged from the room in a series of bunny hops. She looked as if she was stepping on hot coals.

"A rat!" she squealed as she raced towards the staircase. Next Ricardo appeared, closely followed by the children. It was the first time they had been up as far as the attic. Ricardo looked disconcerted, as if he hadn't the faintest idea of where Rosa might have seen this rat, nor what on earth he'd do were he unlucky enough also to catch sight of it, but the children, egged on by the revulsion of the older members of the family – and most of all by their father, now that neither Señor or Señora Blinder showed the least sign of life – ran to and fro like a horde of banshees.

María was terrified they might discover the loft. If they did, it'd be hard to contain them. Luckily, Ricardo waved his arms energetically and made jokes, ordering them to be quiet. The children obeyed.

"It was here," said Rosa, who had just come back in.

She sounded calm: the incident no longer affected her to the least degree. Once the initial shock had passed, she had come back upstairs again, because either Señor or Señora Blinder had asked her to do so, or because she was intent upon rat-catching. In any case, it was highly likely that this wasn't the first rat she had ever seen in the house.

"Where?" asked Ricardo.

Rosa waved in the direction of the bedroom.

"But it's gone now…" she said deceptively, "it left that-away…"

"Children, children," summoned Ricardo, calling his kids, now heading in the direction Rosa had indicated: it afforded a good pretext to flee.

María had closed the door, and was following the scene through the keyhole. The perspective meant that he had too wide a field of vision, but he was able to discern Ricardo and Rosa speaking to one another:

"Fine, if that's the way it is…" said Ricardo, shrugging his shoulders.

"It will soon put in another appearance…" said Rosa.

Ricardo didn't say another word. He signalled to the kids, and the three of them set off down the stairs in single file. In the midst of all this Ricardo, suddenly animated, stretched out his fingers, let out a grunt, then ran after his kids, who accepted his little game, and rapidly got away from him: they ran far faster than he did.

Rosa locked the bedroom door, pocketed the key and followed them down.

17

Up in the attic there was a passage in the shape of an L. Opening off it there were seven bedrooms, a study, a playroom (converted into a loft), an ironing room, a bathroom and two toilets, as well as an enormous open garret, so deserted that María had once nicknamed it "Africa". All in all, it was no trouble for him to set himself up in a different room (even though, when Rosa locked the door and took the key with her, for an instant he felt as if he had been "left out on the street").

He selected the last bedroom on the left-hand side. He could scarcely summon the courage to part the venetian blinds once more: if he had, he would have been able to see that he was much closer to the street corner than before. For the time being, however, he devoted himself to analysing his room: it had the same measurements as the last, an identical bed, situated in the same position as before, and with a similar mattress. He sat himself down, tried it out, looked around him… There was no wardrobe, just a cupboard, and an occasional table, positioned against a wall next to the bed, with three empty drawers and an old round sticker with the rubric *Apple* (referencing the Beatles) stuck to the door. Surely a maid's former bedroom, hip for her times…

If the rat had behaved in the same manner with Rosa as it had the first time he saw it (racing around in a circle, giving the impression that it was on the point of escape, then returning to its point of departure) it was now most likely that it was locked up in the room. Why had Rosa taken the key away in her pocket? None of the remaining six bedrooms were under lock and key. Why had she locked that one in particular? During the final months of their marriage, his parents had slept in separate rooms, and any time one or other of them left the house, they locked their bedroom door and took the key away. They had nothing to hide: most likely they did it to underline their rejection of the other party. The problem there was that they only had two bedrooms in the house, his parents' and his own, which his mother had moved into, meaning that whenever she left the house he couldn't get back into his own room. On some occasions, she would only return late at night. María would wake up in the morning in his own bed only because his mother would carry him up there in the small hours, gathering him up from the cane armchair in the dining room where he had fallen asleep. At other times, if it got too late, his father would take pity on him and invite him to come and wait in his bed, but that happened only on rare occasions, and he was always woken up and moved on as soon as his father heard the front door open.

18

It was on 3rd January, while Ricardo and Rita were packing the cases and the youngest children were staring at the television screen, that Esteban tiptoed into Rosa's room.

Rosa's reaction on seeing him come in was one of surprise. She asked him to leave, but Esteban said something in a low voice, a long sentence which resonated like a hiss, and which seemed to convince her to let him stay there. A silence followed. Then, whispers interrupted by odd eruptions of giggles, and the sound of footsteps pattering across the floor, as if Esteban had run over to Rosa and had just caught her in his arms…

For a moment, only Rosa spoke. She seemed to be speaking in chorus:

"Esteban!"

"No, Esteban, someone might come in!…"

"Be quiet…"

"Quiet now, Esteban…"

"No!"

"I told you already, no!"

"Look at you now, eh?"

Now it was Esteban's turn to speak while Rosa remained silent.

"I'm leaving."

"I thought that… perhaps…"

"OK. I'm sorry."

Silence.

"Are you cross with me?" (Esteban.)

"No…" (Rosa.)

"Are you sure?" asked Esteban.

Rosa nodded, yes.

"But I'm cross with *you*, really cross," Esteban said. Rosa raised her eyes to look at him. Esteban added: "Do you really think I don't know you're going out with that stupid fat guy with the dimpled flesh?"

"That has nothing to do with it, Esteban. In any case…"

Silence.

136

"In any case, what?"

"Nothing."

"Come on, out with it, out with it! I'm too young for you? Is that what you were going to say? Well, it didn't seem that way to you last year…"

"That was a game."

"Sure."

"Honestly, I mean it."

"My therapist doesn't happen to think it was a game."

"You told your therapist about it?"

"Obviously. And you've no idea how hard I had to plead to stop him from telling my parents everything too."

"Oh no…"

"The old fellow strung me a line of legal terms. I can still feel the icy sweat running down my spine, as I felt then, I promise you. That's how I felt with him, believe me. Not with you. With you it was different…"

"Why did you tell him all this?"

"Because I pay him, obviously!"

"That's mad…"

"Don't pursue the point, it's not taking us anywhere. And I can guarantee that this year I'm going back to London in far worse shape than last year. Since I've been here, I've had no shut-eye at all… Listen Rosa, I don't want to hassle you, I don't want you to believe I'm telling you all this to put pressure on you in order to make you do anything at all you don't want. It's just that you made me so happy when…"

"Don't cry…"

"OK. Let's forget about it. It's not your fault. My behavioural problems, my sudden rages, my night-mares… what do you have to do with any of all that? It was my fault to let myself go along with it. I've been an idiot…"

"Esteban…"

"I'm leaving. We'll see each other again next year. I really hope I'll have forgotten all about you by then…"

"Where are your mum and dad?"

"Packing the cases…"

"Have the Señores come home?"

"My grandparents?"

"Yes."

"No, they're still not back."

"We'll have to be really quick."

"Whatever you say, my love."

"But promise me something first. When you return next year, we'll move on from all this."

"I promise."

"Swear to me, by God."

"Come over to me, and stop right here…"

At that point, María heard the voices of the younger children approaching, and scarcely had time to conceal himself. His heart was pounding heavily, with what sounded like an echo, so it seemed as if he had two hearts rather than one.

The children came running down the corridor. They were uttering hysterical shrieks. At once Esteban emerged from the room, adjusting his belt: he looked pale and scared. The children swept him along ahead of them. They didn't seem surprised at having bumped into their big brother so suddenly; instead they were anxious to free themselves from him and carry on zooming around. But Esteban grabbed them with one arm and shook them violently. He was on the point of ordering them to leave immediately when Ricardo unexpectedly appeared. He came along roaring like a beast, with his hands extended like paws and a monstrous expression on his face.

Esteban saw him and smiled.

"I caught them!" he said, feigning he was joining in.

Ricardo shrugged his shoulders and let his arms fall to his sides.

"What on earth are you doing up here?" he asked.

"I'm allowed to take a turn about the house?" replied Esteban.

Ricardo considered for a moment.

"Come on you lot, the game is over," he said slowly. "We're going."

"Already?" asked Esteban.

"Yes, already," his father told him.

It was an order.

Esteban joined his brother and sister in an ill-tempered huff, with an expression of a man sorely *interruptus* on his face.

Ricardo tracked them with his eyes as the three of them passed him by, heading for the staircase. Then he followed them down, with little tight steps, like an animal herding its young.

19

"Rosa, it's me…"

"Ah, María…"

"All well?"

"How do I know…"

"What's up?"

"Just about everything…"

"Tell me about it…"

"No, leave it out…"

"Come on, tell me, my love, don't be an idiot! What happened to you?"

"Where are you?"

"Don't start over with that…"

"The Señores' children were staying here with their own kids, I'm not sure if I told you the last time we spoke, but…" Rosa interrupted herself.

"But?…"

"Nothing, that's all. I've no idea what I was going to tell you…"

"Was there some problem?"

"Who with?"

"With them? Or with one or another of them, I don't know…"

"No…"

"From the way you put it, it seemed as if there was. You're not going to tell me that one of them made a pass at you?" persisted María. Rosa changed the subject.

"Do you know what I wanted to tell you? That the other day I was outside the house and all of a sudden I turned round and… you won't believe this, you'll think I've gone crazy… it seemed to me there was someone upstairs, in one of the rooms, on the top floor, a person…"

"So what?" asked María after a pause. "No doubt it was somebody from the house…"

"Well yes, possibly," said Rosa, suddenly deflated. "I went straight upstairs but I couldn't find anyone at all… There was a rat there, though, you know? Yuck – and I've gone and forgotten to put some rat poison down."

"You'd put poison down to catch a rat?"

"The Señora told me to. Seems fair enough. If I spotted one, it can only be because there are more. And that's the first time I've ever seen one. When I first came to work here, I thought the place would be full of mice, but apparently not. That's the first time I've ever seen one. No, that's a lie, there was one other occasion. But it was a really long time ago… María, why don't you come over here? Where on earth are you?"

This time it was María who changed the subject.

"And the fat guy you told me was pursuing you last time we spoke?" he enquired.

Once more Rosa switched the topic of conversation:

"Oh you've no idea: last time the phone kept being engaged and I went upstairs to see if I'd replaced the receiver properly, and when I touched it I found it was all warm! Or tepid, as if someone had just been using it… As if someone had been using it right up until the time I got there…"

María felt gooseflesh prickle his skin. He glanced rapidly around him, looking for a cloth or a napkin he could use to hold the earpiece from now on, by way of forestalling Rosa's assumptions, should it cross her mind that it could have been him using the phone, and that she should go upstairs and check whether it was still warm or not. But there was nothing lying around he could use to wrap the receiver in. The house seemed as stripped bare as he was. For the first time since he'd been living there, he observed that the principal materials used to build the villa were marble, wood and metal. The only fibres in sight were in the carpets and curtains. Exactly the opposite of his own home, where there were rags and scraps of fabric lying all over the place…

He was left no option but to hold the receiver between two fingers, his index finger and thumb, as if the phone were suddenly on fire or had changed into an object of disgust.

"Aren't you being ever so slightly paranoid?"

"Yes, it's possible... I don't know, it seemed to me..."

"It's so incredibly hot, if you think about it..."

"Only not here. Here the heat only comes with the autumn. Do you know that out to sea... I read it the other day in *Selections*... do you know why the sea is cold by day and warm at night?"

"Why?"

"Because the sun warms it up during the day. Then it gets late. The sun stays there all day warming and warming it up, and you get to feel the benefit at night. Because at night the same thing happens. At night the water cools down little by little, and you can feel it's properly cold by the next day."

"Have you ever been to the coast at Mar del Plata? It's incredible that I've never even asked you that before..."

"No. And you? I've never asked you about it either..."

"Yes, I went there once, quite a while ago. It's really pretty there."

"I guess you've been and taken a photo with those two big polar bears you see on the way into the resort..."

"They're lions. Sea lions. No, I never took a picture, I didn't have a camera. It was because I didn't go there on my holidays: I went there to work. We built a skyscraper over thirty storeys high, thirty-five maybe, I can't remember now. A real monster. God it was hot! When you looked down from on top, it was like being on top of an anthill!"

"And on Sundays? Did you also work on Sundays?"

"No, on Sundays I actually got to go to the resort. Once you went down into it, it didn't seem like such an anthill. You got used to it."

"And was I right or wrong, about when the water got cold?"

142

"Sometimes it did. One Sunday it was, another not so much. Do you know who I saw there one day?"

"Was it Cristian Castro?"

"No, unfortunately. It was Juan Leyrado. He wore a little beret and sunglasses, and he had a belly, bulging eyes, a T-shirt, I don't know what else. He looked like a Martian, but I still recognized him. And another time I saw Adolfo Bioy Casares, I don't know if you're familiar with him…"

"No…"

"He's a writer. How strange you not knowing who he is: he's a very famous author. I've seen him in a heap of photos."

"I didn't realize…"

"That's a pity. You see someone like that and you recognize a gentleman, a dandy, a real señor. I mean it seriously, he's a proper intellectual. Now, if I'm not mistaken, he's dead… But on that occasion he was there, sitting by a canvas windbreak, watching the people go by, dressed to the nines, and with a hat, you ought to have seen it. Even at a hundred yards, he looked something else. And guess what – I pass by and I take a look at him, and the guy takes a look back at me, then sweeps off his hat and greets me!"

"Did he know you?"

"No of course not, how could he? Don't be ridiculous. But he looked at me and tipped his hat at me, I swear to God. And from that very moment I loved him. I don't usually like to speak in such terms, but yes: I loved him. And then I was left there just thinking… Don't you think that the government will have to make itself responsible for writers and for their children's future? What I say is – what would it cost the government to put half a million *pesos* in the bank for its artists, so they could

143

write away quietly, without worrying about the future? What's half a million to the government? Nothing, no more than loose change. I did the sums. The State gives them some spare cash, and they deliver a book. What do you think?"

"What do I know about it? We're here breaking our backs all day long too…"

"But that's not the same, my darling: we're the working class."

"Ah well, all the more reason, then. Why would the government be about to award money to artists so they can dance the night away on a stage, and not give us – the workers – anything at all, having to dance to their tune morning, noon and night. On top of which, nobody even thinks of applauding *us*!"

"Rosa, I don't feel like an argument…"

Silence.

"One day I'd love to take you to the Mar del Plata…" said María.

Another silence.

"Hello?" asked María.

"Where are you?"

"You've already asked me that a thousand times over, Rosa. And I've already told you I can't let you know. You'll just have to get used to the idea that I am where I am… that I love you just as much as ever… and… well, you know how things are."

"No. That's just it, I don't."

"Tell me about the big guy. Who is he?"

"No one. It doesn't matter. That's enough."

"Are you annoyed with me?"

"No."

"It sounds to me as if you are."

"Are you in prison?"

144

"No."

"I can't believe what you're putting me through… and I'm getting really tired of it."

"Don't say that, my darling!"

"But José María, what do you want me to say to you, if you won't tell me anything?"

"Don't call me José María: it sounds as if you don't know who I am. In any case, you aren't offering me any explanations either…"

"What am I not offering you any explanations about?"

"I asked you about the fat guy – and nothing. You tell me absolutely nothing. Who is he?"

"You come and visit me here, and I'll tell you."

"You know, you're a really good negotiator! You should be a lawyer, you should."

Silence.

"Withdraw what you said about being tired of me."

"I never said that I was tired of you. You misheard me. I told you I'm beginning to tire of this whole novel you're spinning me."

"Me too. Would you prefer it if we hung up?"

"You want to hang up?"

"I asked you first…"

"If you want to hang up, then do so," said Rosa after a pause.

And after another pause, María hung up, offended.

20

He didn't call her again until the end of the summer. Throughout those months he lived like a recluse (which is really saying something, referring to someone as reclusive as he), in a miniaturized version of a world of normal activities. Gymnastic exercises, reading books and, best of all, his nocturnal excursions in search of food were still his major pastimes: he suspended his walks, stopped taking an interest in movements around the house, avoided listening in on the Blinders' conversations and concentrated all his efforts on not knowing anything about Rosa's life, just as if he wanted to forget all about her.

He was wounded. The image he had in his head of Álvaro raping her tortured him... The fact that Esteban was on the point of making out with her (probably for the second time), also that the "big guy" or the "fat man" was still calling her and presumably meeting up with her on the street pained him, but he was most of all hurt by the tone in which Rosa had addressed him during their last conversation, a dry tone that deliberately excluded him.

Why had she spoken to him in that manner?

Whereas it was true he never told her where he was, it was also true that she had her suspicions that he was a prisoner, when he kept calling and swearing his love for her. Did his voice and his vows not affect her, were they stripped of all meaning by the simple lack of his presence? How come she could fall for Cristian Castro without ever having met him, and be unable to feel the same for him? He was pretty sure that if Cristian Castro suddenly appeared and told her: "Stay faithful to me for the next twenty years, and I'll come and collect you when my career is over," she would have been absolutely true to him.

He couldn't exactly ask her direct, precise questions; nor had she ever offered any sign of confiding the secrets of her private life in him. In one sense, she was deceiving him. She said she was in love with him, but she hadn't said a single word about Álvaro raping her, or about Esteban's seduction, even about the "big guy" and his intentions. On the contrary: she was always avoiding them and pushing them aside. Were he really a prisoner, as she assumed, was that sufficient cause, in no more than a couple of months, for her to entertain at least three suitors, including one rapist?

It pained him to be unable to say that he was living with her...

Finally, one afternoon, he realized what that tone was in Rosa's voice, which had so offended him. Rosa addressed him like that because she had grown used to those mysterious little chats with him, not because she either didn't desire or didn't care for them. But then, just as he was disposed to forgive her and call her up again, he looked out of the first-floor window and saw Rosa downstairs with Israel.

He felt such intense loathing as he recognized the man, and not because he was wearing one of his hideous rugby shirts. María had forced himself to believe it wasn't actually Israel, but some other man. The shirt, it had to be said, made his hackles rise and obliged him to confront reality: Israel, his enemy, the provocative idiot who aeons ago had hit him in front of Rosa, this was the "fat guy", the "big boy". His attitude – the attitude of the two of them – stopped there in the doorway to the tradesmen's entrance, left no room for doubt: romance was in the air. The smiles, the flirtatious manner in which looks were raised or dropped shyly downwards...

María ground his teeth and his eyes filled with tears.

Israel gave Rosa a kiss on her cheek and started to move off, still saying something to her, no doubt "I'll call you" or "let's talk about it later", that would fit the gesture he was making with his hand, with his little finger and thumb spread over his face. Rosa nodded. Then she closed and locked the door, and walked back a few yards, staring thoughtfully at the ground. María wanted to believe that Rosa was pondering whether what she was doing was the right thing... Rosa must have decided that it was, since a smile suddenly lit up her face, and she ran the remaining distance to the kitchen skipping like a teenager.

It was horrible, the worst possible betrayal. Now, just when he had come to understand everything, he could believe none of it. He decided to disappear, disappear into the interior of his own disappearance, before he met Rosa. He didn't hate her. But he could never forgive her the relationship with Israel. From that moment on, he would *really and truly* lock himself away. He wished to know nothing more about her.

A few days earlier, Rosa had scattered rat poison throughout the attic rooms. It was in cubic granules, like large grains of rock salt, laid out in little mounds in every corner. He had gathered them all up and scattered them in the toilet grating a few days later, to give the impression that the rat had eaten them. During the days he lived with the poison in his room, he had never noticed its smell. Not a single grain of poison remained in sight, but now its smell pervaded everywhere.

21

His isolation was almost complete. In the ground-floor living room there was a stereo system with a radio, but he obviously couldn't switch it on. The Walkman, lacking headphones, was of no use to him, and the

Blinders didn't subscribe to a daily newspaper. The only publication which arrived regularly was *Selections from the Reader's Digest*, which on one occasion he had leafed through in the Blinders' bedroom without any of what he read catching his attention.

He knew who was president because he'd heard his name used, but this was now so long ago he was unsure whether he was still in power. There were three television sets in the house: one in the ground-floor living room; another in Señora Blinder's bedroom; and the third in Rosa's room. Señor Blinder always switched on the living-room television, and the only thing he watched were Argentine and European football matches. Señora Blinder watched films in her bedroom, and Rosa watched soaps and all kinds of celebrity-gossip programmes, but he had never felt secure watching television behind closed doors, because the sound would have prevented him hearing whether Rosa or Señora Blinder had left the building. That meant the only news he had heard from the outside world was that emanating from the living-room television set.

There Señor Blinder watched almost nothing but football matches. On one occasion, María gathered that the United States had attacked Iraq, and that a woman in a country house somewhere in Buenos Aires province, an upper-class woman, had been murdered, possibly by a family member, although an extensive investigation had thus far failed to find the assassin. The war and the rural crime – with all the interminable discussions and conjectures they elicited – were the only subjects which, in the course of many years, had proved substantially more attractive than football.

Perhaps Señor Blinder was a lawyer, or a doctor, and read the paper in his office or his surgery. If that were not the case, you might conclude that Señor Blinder had turned his back on the world, reducing it to a series of football stadiums. On whom was he turning his back, then? On the house and on Rosa.

He spent the greater part of the day (and all night) locked in his room. With the penknife he had stolen from Ricardo, he began to carve and construct boats and planes and some animals, using matches and soap. They were tiny sculptures measuring three to six inches in height, which took him days to complete, and which he hid in the attic when he had finished them.

He let his beard and his hair grow long, as well as the nail on the index finger of his right hand, which he used to make the soap sculptures. From time to time he went out to get some light and air on his face – a pyramid of glass in the middle of the floor – and there he lay down with his eyes closed, as if on a sun lounger. Susceptible, dumb, naked.

After months of nudity, without the constant friction of the rough, poor-quality materials he had worn throughout his life, his skin was softer than it had ever been. Nor had his fingers ever been more sensitive. How many millions of blows and small cuts to the hand had he endured in the daily tasks which he now set himself? How may pounds of chalk dust and earth had he inhaled? When he was wearing boots or shoes his heels were covered in a tough layer of skin, almost like a slipper. Ever since he had been going barefoot, forever walking on marble, polished wood or on carpets, the hard patches had diminished and almost disappeared.

He repressed the imaginary conversations with Rosa, yet she reappeared frequently in his dreams. One night he dreamed they were both off to the Mar del Plata, and on another that they were on their way home, as if in dream worlds there could also be a continuity between one thing and the next, one dream and the next, until the holidays vanished in smoke and only the travel remained. In the same way, his sexual life had reduced to the maximum degree. One night he dreamed he was making love with Rosa, but in later dreams she only appeared making love with Israel. Israel was tattooed with the image of a life-sized eagle on his back, the tips of its spread wings nudging the backs of his thighs.

Gradually rage gave way to disappointment, and finally disappointment stopped pressing the magic button of desire, extinguishing it: he stopped masturbating, either in his dreams or in reality. (Only once did he dream he was masturbating. Such an image had never previously entered his dreams).

However much against his will, it was inevitable that a certain amount of information would filter through to him about what was going on in the house. These were really more in the way of references or signs, and fairly minor ones too – the slam of a door, long hours of total silence, someone calling a name in a loud voice – permitting him to form an overview – however little he intended to do so – a bird's-eye view, really, of the course the Blinders' marriage was running (from bad to worse) and the state of Rosa's spirits (good). This information irritated him, for the least amount of it evoked awkward questions. Was Rosa seeing Israel *every day of the week* now? Was she in love with him? Didn't it count that Israel was a poor little rich kid, who probably just wanted to take her to bed, but with whom there was no future relationship, and who was bound to make her suffer? Didn't she realize that no doubt Israel was laughing at her behind her back, in the club with his other crude friends from the *barrio*, telling them every last detail of "the titbit I've nibbled"?

The same applied to her future at work. One morning he had overheard a shouting match between Señor and Señora Blinder: they were in deep financial trouble. The villa had been up for sale for years now. But, unless some country wanted to buy it up in order to install their embassy there, it was, given its incredibly high value, virtually impossible to sell. Did Rosa realize her workplace was up for sale? One time long ago, when they had visited a bar after a trip to the cinema, they had talked about the number of new countries appearing on the world map. Rosa failed to understand how it was possible for a country to arise out of nowhere, with territory, inhabitants, a judicial system and a flag, a national anthem and a president. "It's not out of nowhere," he had told her, "they're becoming autonomous. The land and the people are already there, all they have to do is to compose an anthem and elect a president." Was Rosa aware that at any moment someone could turn up and buy the villa as the ambassadorial residence of one of these new countries? What would then become of her? Or of him?

He had already been over this question a number of times. Whenever he started thinking of her, he ended up thinking of himself. But Rosa would have good references, that was beyond doubt; she could obtain a job in some other grand mansion, or maybe even here in fact, the embassy of that new country, only in this case she would have become a foreigner in her own country. Could foreigners work in the embassy of another land? And what would happen if they took on and employed Israel's parents? That would be terrible. Rosa might become pregnant by Israel and repeat his own personal history...

Over four decades earlier María's mother had worked as a domestic servant in the house of Governor Castro's intendant. And people muttered under their breath – although their whispering had reached as far as him – that her son was really fathered by the intendant.

The man whom María had always called "dad" was blond, freckled and short; nothing about one of them resembled the other. Nor did he in any way resemble his mother. When the rumour reached him, he was already grown, and the intendant had died years earlier, so he could hardly go and meet him and make the comparison. For years the subject had gnawed away at him, but he had never dared to mention it. From time to time in the village he'd meet an elderly and aristocratic lady, who would look at him oddly: she always went about with a vacant expression until she set eyes on him. Then she would seem to pull herself together and wake up. She was the intendant's widow.

The very same day his mother went off with another man, María went into his father's room and put the question to him. Well, he didn't put it directly: first he went in and hung around awhile, saying nothing.

A few minutes later, his father – who was stretched out on a couch staring at the television set – averted his gaze and looked at him:

"What are you crying for?" he asked.

María was crying because his mother had left. But he answered that he was crying because he'd heard he wasn't really his son.

The father raised himself up on his elbows.

"Who told you that?" he asked angrily.

"The kids. They say I'm the son of the intendant… Is that true?"

"No."

"So why do?…"

153

"You tell those kids to stop talking rubbish," interrupted his father, rolling over onto his back on the couch once more.

He hadn't thought about it again since then. He remembered the incident because of Rosa, but also because it was his birthday: his forty-first birthday.

He wasn't sure of the precise date. He had taken up residence in the villa on the 26th or 27th September, so today could as well be the 9th or the 10th April. ...

He uncorked the champagne he had stolen over Christmas, and had concealed in the attic, and drank about a third of the bottle in tiny sips, without ceremony, his eyes fixed on the wall across the room.

It began to turn cold. He remembered what he had told Rosa about the sea temperatures... It was already two weeks since the cold had descended on the city. People were going out dressed in their overcoats and were hurrying on their way. The trees down in the garden were starting to shed their leaves. The lawn had stopped growing and, all along a lane which extended like a long black thread, the ants were hastening along with their enormous bundles of sky-blue, yellow and red.

He hadn't seen anything of all this. Yet he knew it was exactly like this.

22

Love wears a woman's face... The Catwoman... The Fugitive... Combat... View over Biondi... those were some of the programmes which, in another era, his parents had fought over. These weren't merely arguments over who would watch which, but actual fights. They always started with an argument; then, almost always, they'd turn into shouts and, more than likely, sessions of pushing and shoving. His father listened to records by Pérez Prado. His mother to Leonardo Favio. His mother smoked. His father didn't. His mother worked. His father didn't. One point in his father's favour: he cooked. But his mother disliked the stews on which his father expended such considerable efforts.

Television, music, work, cooking, anything could become the pretext for a fight. The drawback (if one could call it that) was that the fights weren't a means of staying together, as in those relationships where love has transmuted into a permanent safety valve. His parents' battles were born of nothing more than mutual intolerance, mutual antipathy. They hated one another, full stop.

His father slept an enormous amount, by day or night. His mother was an insomniac...

It was years since he'd last seen either of them, but at least he knew where to find his... if he truly was *his father*. What on earth did this matter to him *now*?

Then his eyes glazed over – with loathing, not with pain – and he saw the rat.

Was it the same rat, his friend, his companion?

María stayed stock-still, as though made of air and light, one cheek resting against one of the glass walls. He widened his eyes when he felt someone (something) looking at him, and saw it. The rat was three or four yards away from him. It maintained a certain distance from the wall, and as if no longer needing to hug the skirting board, as if in the very act of looking at him it had evolved – or leaped – into an intermediate state somewhere between that of its own species and of his.

In fact the rat was regarding him as a dog would. María could even see that now it was gently waving its tail. But – was it the *same one*?

Had it survived the dose of poison? Or had it died and this was its wife, who came to resume the friendship? They looked at each other for a long time, both of them utterly immobile. Until all of a sudden the rat took a step towards him. The tiny step forwards of a humanized rat.

"Yes, it's me," it seemed to be saying.

María thought it would have to be far easier for a rat to recognize a man than for a man to recognize a rat.

He let one arm drop to his side, quietly extending his hand along the floor, inviting the rat to approach him. Then the rat made a half-turn and fled at full speed.

María closed his eyes again.

Yes, in the end it was a stroke of luck that his mother hadn't wanted to see him again. Neither him nor his fake father, or however much of a real father he might have been.

23

"Rosa?…"
Silence.
He hung up.

24

He had never imagined a winter indoors, inside a villa, could be that tough. He retrieved his work clothes from his knapsack, and wore them all at once: two shirts, two pairs of trousers, pants, socks, and he added a jumper, belonging to Señor Blinder, that he'd stolen one afternoon from the top shelf of his wardrobe.

The walls were literally freezing. The metal slats of the venetian blinds, however, had gone to the other extreme: they were so cold they were burning. Sometimes in the mornings, but most of all at night, the wind made a noise like a raging banshee, inserting fine blades into the narrowest cracks which the air – its brother – would have been unable to penetrate.

The lights on the ground floor were always left on. Sequestered in his room, María did his daily exercises: a hundred arm flexes, a hundred abdominal crunches – slowly, one after the other, giving each equal weight, equal concentration, just as much as he would have bestowed on every kiss he gave Rosa.

He no longer missed her, yet not a minute went by without his thinking of her.

And he no longer wanted to see her. At times he even turned his back on her, when she came upstairs to clean the room, wash out the toilets, run the vacuum cleaner over the floors or wipe the windows (occasions on which she always, like any other woman doing the same thing, seemed so utterly absented). The phantom desired only to remain a phantom. Wherever it had hidden itself away, each time Rosa came upstairs to clean the attic, he (religiously) turned his back on her, as if it were some part of his feng shui. María's adoration for her was so great that he had had to become a mystic in order to deny her without dying himself.

25

This "relapse" (the telephone call during which he could manage no more than to say her name and, after a silence which said no more than "?…", hang up) took place on 7th June. From then on, nothing more occurred to encourage him to ring her. Rather, it would have been a distraction.

He was truly in an altered state of being. His body still expressed it better than his soul or his psychology: his very fibres were as stretched as if they were all nerve endings, absorbed within an aura of contained force, with the briefest of shivers here and there, from top to toe, resembling nervous tics or miniature explosions. The contrast between his appearance and some of his pastimes (reading best-sellers, carving soap sculptures) could not have been greater. Intellectually, he was light years behind an average child, even in terms of wisdom: he existed as if in a glove whose extremities both touched and were touched (the butterfly and the petal). This was he, who a year earlier would have boasted that he was all *streetwise*…

All his artistry was concentrated in the shape of a soap canoe (without either oars or rowers). Despite this, he had constructed a double invisibility for himself and for everyone else, and all out of (he could hardly bring himself to write the word) spite. His crime obliged him to hide himself away, but his spitefulness made a monk out of him.

26

"Hello, Rosa?"

How long it had been since he had spoken her name! Not even he could believe it.

Rosa, at the other end of the line, was as surprised as he was.

"María?"

"Yes, it's me."

"Oh my God…"

"How are you?"

"Where are you?"

"Forgive me for not ringing you in so long, but I wanted to suggest something to you…" he said. There was a pause, and amid the silence in the house you could hear Rosa's irregular breathing from both ends of the line, sounding like a gasp.

"Would you like to meet me?"

"What happened?" asked Rosa.

For an instant, María was unsure whether her question referred to his invitation, as if the fact of his wanting to see her would necessarily mean that something bad had happened, or whether it was no more than the old question, born of anxiety, which she had repeatedly posed him from the beginning.

He decided it must be the latter and a fragile hint of sadness rippled delicately up his spine: why, in spite of all that had happened, did Rosa still appear to be stuck in the same place? Was this really the only thing that mattered to her?

"Look Rosa," he said, "first of all there's been something I've wanted to say to you for a long time and, for one reason or another, I've kept on forgetting. There's a book called *Your Erroneous Zones*. I want you to read it. Look it out in the villa's library, I'm sure your employers will have a copy. It's called *Your Erroneous Zones*. On the cover there's a picture of a man half-leaning forwards, made up of words. I kept wanting to tell you. It has to be good luck that I've finally remembered it. Now let's get on with talking about ourselves…"

"María? Are you well? Your voice sounds different…"

159

"Did you hear what I told you? Would you like us to meet?"

"Are you serious?"

María nodded.

But Rosa couldn't see him, so she repeated the question:

"Are you serious?"

"Yes," said María. "Would you like us to meet up?"

"What happened?"

They had come back to their starting point. At this point, María could observe the usual circularity of their dialogues, and use it to revise his plan.

Which he did from the beginning.

His resistance to assimilating what had been going on in the house was so great that he knew even less about what by now was impossible to ignore. But one afternoon, five days earlier, he had heard Señora Blinder exclaim:

"Rosa, oh my God!"

That expression awoke his curiosity.

He went downstairs. It was months since he had descended to the first floor in daytime.

Ten minutes later he came back upstairs again. He shut himself in his room and stayed there crouched in a corner. His heart was thumping heavily. Those ten minutes had been sufficient for him to accumulate a sequence of facts and indicators (visual fragments, odd sentences) for him now to create a panorama of the main events of the most recent period, like someone putting their hand in the water and taking out a fistful of earth or sand in order to later analyse the composition of the subsoil.

What he discovered meant that the protective wall he had erected between himself and the house fractured at a stroke:

160

a) Rosa was pregnant;

b) Israel didn't want to know.

The second point filled him with loathing. The first with pain. Rosa pregnant...

Now he had seen for himself. Señora Blinder was standing in front of Rosa. He saw Señora Blinder come in, but Rosa was bisected vertically by the door frame and the only part of her in his line of vision was precisely her abdomen: she was stroking it at a speed more fitting to that of a satisfied customer than of a mother. Maybe it made her ashamed, or maybe she was afraid of what the Señora was about to say... It was a small bump, but it was definitely there. Of this there was absolutely no doubt.

Señora Blinder swivelled on her heels, turning her back on him, and then swung round again, to go towards Rosa, evidently nervous. Rosa allowed a sob to escape her. Señora Blinder put her arms around her.

It was probably the first time she had ever embraced her, since Rosa took a rapid pace backwards, either in fear or surprise. The two then stood outside his field of vision.

He descended a few more steps, and carefully craned his neck forwards. Yes, they were definitely embracing. Actually, only Señora Blinder was really doing the embracing. Rosa's arms were dangling at her sides.

"Who is the father?"

"I can't tell you that, Señora..."

Señora Blinder detached herself and, without letting her go completely, looked her in the eyes. Suddenly she looked very serious, as if Rosa were playing her a wild card or making a bad joke.

"Rosa," she said, "I could have told you to pack your bag and move on, now couldn't I? Yet, in spite of all this, I'm still here and I want to help you."

"If you tell me to, I'll leave right away…"

"Don't you ever say such a thing in front of me again! Are we clear?" Señora Blinder replied, making the sign of the cross.

"Yes, Señora. Nor would I have…"

"That's enough. Let's begin again. Who is the father?"

"Israel, Señora."

"Who is Israel?"

"The fellow who lives here, on the corner, Señora… He lives at number 1525, on the fourth floor."

"Who lives there on the fourth floor?"

"Israel, Señora. I'm sure you know him actually, he told me that you always greet one another as you pass by on the street, and that one time you stopped and spoke to him. Do you remember the boyfriend I once had, called María?"

"María?"

"José María, but I called him María. Israel told me that on one occasion he spoke to you over that matter with the police, who came round to check if…"

"Israel Vargas!"

"Yes, Señora."

"Unbelievable…"

Señora Blinder made another half-turn and crossed the bottom of the staircase, going towards her room, walking slowly and thoughtfully. María backed off and managed to escape by a hair's breadth. A second later, Rosa also passed by. No doubt, Señora Blinder had signalled for her to draw closer.

"Very well, we need to talk to him," said Señora Blinder. "I assume he will take responsibility…"

María didn't listen any further. He retreated one step at a time, like a solid shadow, and shut himself in his room. His walls had just collapsed in on him.

His head was spinning. His nausea was not the result of having been "absent" for so long: it was his re-entry into that world which shattered him. Rosa pregnant... and by none other than Israel. If only Señora Blinder had thrown her out onto the street... After all it had been a long time since he'd even thought of her... He would have preferred to wake one morning to the news that Rosa was no longer there than to learn of her pregnancy.

He had worked hard with all his might to forget her and, in the process, had transformed himself into another man. And he was the better for it. Of the old María, he had conserved the agility – even though he was no longer as strong, nor as robust – and all the rest had changed. He was more spiritual: he could have borne anything. His goal in staying in the house was no longer to escape imprisonment. This was a matter he no longer even thought about. It would have been more appropriate for him simply to disappear. It was enough for him to set foot upon this peak of human indifference for a pregnancy to come along and sabotage it all! Rage and pain rose through his body like hot flames. He felt indignant, disgusted and at the same time fearful. Had he really learned *anything* about either himself or the house?

What about Señora Blinder, for example? What did he really know about her? He knew nothing at all beyond what he could imagine. The proof was that Señora Blinder had just demonstrated herself to be gentle, understanding and even fair towards Rosa, rather than cold and rejecting. That very night Señora Blinder had even, after telling the news to her husband (who was indeed cold and scornful), defended Rosa with a set of arguments as moving as they were fruitless, a force of nature before which her husband could do little else but weaken:

"Do what you like."

The next day it appeared that Señora Blinder had indeed gone to speak to Israel. Rosa anxiously awaited her return. When she got back, Señora Blinder slipped an arm about her waist and swept her out of María's sight, saying:

"We're going to have to take charge of this ourselves. To start with…"

At that instant, María took his decision. The same night he rose and got dressed, went downstairs with his shoes in his hand, took the key to the kitchen door, opened it, went out, locked it again from the outside, put on his shoes, crossed the side garden to the kitchen gate, opened it, went out, locked it again from the outside, crossed the street and disappeared into the darkness. He was absolutely certain no one had seen him.

It must have been about three in the morning, and it was very cold. The streets were deserted. From time to time a car passed by in the distance. María had the sensation he had been walking those streets the previous day… but at another hour. He didn't register that he was out of doors until he went into the locksmith's. In some sense, being outside was hardly all that important, after all. What mattered was being inside. It even (in a *barrio* hitherto unknown to him) seemed curious that he had gone straight to the nearest locksmith, a locksmith which remained open round the clock, as if he'd ended up knowing the *barrio* from within the villa.

A man advanced in years, with the aspect of a retired crook, looked suspiciously at him all the time he made a copy of the key. María held his gaze. (Between them there flashed the sparks made by the key-cutter.) Eventually

María made his way back to the villa. Once inside the tradesmen's entrance, he took off his shoes and repeated the same careful actions he had performed in leaving, with a brief pause in the kitchen to select his dinner.

That was on 12th August. The rest followed naturally. Next morning, on 13th August, he would call her by phone and tell her he wanted to see her. He could only leave the house at dawn, which was what he would do that very 13th August, and spend the night out on the street until he went to his assignation with Rosa – some time either in the morning or the afternoon – in some place yet to be determined, after which he would bid her farewell and return to the house at dawn on the 14th August. He knew very well what he was going to say to her. It would mark the end of their going round in circles.

"Don't spin me any more twisters, Rosa. Would you like us to meet, yes or no?"

"Yes."

"Well?"

"Well… where would you like to meet up?"

"The little hotel on the Bajo?"

"I don't think so, María. Now that things are…" she interrupted herself.

"Different?" finished María sadly.

Rosa paused a while and, as was her habit each time a difficult question came up, changed the subject:

"Would you like us to meet in La Cigale?"

"So what's wrong with the little hotel, that you don't want to meet there any more? I'm not about to bite you…"

"Of course I know you're not going to bite me," Rosa laughed (mirthlessly). "The problem is that…"

"Forget it. I'll be waiting for you at the entrance."

"Of La Cigale?"

"Of the little hotel."

"Don't you prefer La Cigale?"

"No. I don't want to meet in La Cigale. I don't want anyone to see us. I'll wait for you at the entrance to the little hotel at… well, you tell me."

"At five o'clock."

"As late as that?" María said, then straight away realized that it was all the same to him, whatever time they met: in any case he was going to have to spend the rest of the day out on the street, until night fell. "It's fine. At five o'clock sharp," he added, "I'll wait for you at the entrance. See you tomorrow."

"María?"

"Yes?"

"No, nothing…"

A pause followed.

"See you tomorrow," repeated María.

Rosa asked him a question:

"Are you all right?"

"I'm OK. What about you?" said María.

"Me too."

"Good. I'm glad for you…"

Another pause.

"Good, until tomorrow…"

"Until tomorrow, my…" and María sharply interrupted himself.

27

Rosa didn't show.

María spent twenty minutes waiting for her in the doorway to the little hotel, another ten minutes on the opposite pavement, and still a further twenty minutes in pacing to and fro.

He was beside himself with rage.

He was on the point of leaving when he suddenly caught sight of Israel.

It was such a monstrous coincidence that it could only have occurred in order to justify and compensate for the fact that Rosa had stood him up.

Israel was standing by a newspaper kiosk, studying the cover of a magazine. He had one hand stuffed in his pocket, where he was jingling his keys or some loose change, while the other hand was busy for real: it scratched the nape of his neck, his nose, adjusted his rugby shirt, held down the magazine cover each time the wind lifted it… María didn't need to pause to think. He crossed the street and went straight over to him.

He stopped beside him. At that very instant Israel had finished reading and had straightened himself up ready to move on, but the cover of another magazine, hung directly below the first, caught his attention. The first one was all about weapons, the second about hunting. María smelled his odour – a powerful blast of pine combined with armpit sweat – and examined the stubble of his hairline, recently trimmed around his nape and over his ears. His neck was considerably wider than his head and his ears even smaller than his eyes. The kiosk's owner surfaced, counting a roll of banknotes. Israel pulled himself together and went slowly on his way.

María followed him. It was a Friday and the Bajo was full of cars hell-bent on escaping the city. People came and went, some hurrying too rapidly and others making no haste at all, as if they were all equally lost. Israel proceeded in a straight line. He held his elbows out, obliging anyone coming towards him to move out of his way, but it was clear he had no particular destination in mind. He was taking a stroll, perhaps killing time until it was his customary dinner time. Twilight was already setting in, but fortunately Israel continued following a path that took him away from his house, towards which María could not have followed him, for fear of being spotted by one of the builders at his old building site, or by the doorman, or even by Rosa... He was forgetting that by now it would be very difficult for anyone to recognize him: he was thin, pale, with long hair down to his shoulders, and several months' growth of beard. So it was that Israel, awoken by María's glare fixed on the back of his neck, turned round and stared back at him.

They had reached a street corner. María, who had followed behind at a distance of six or seven yards, held his gaze as he caught up with him, without allowing his pace to show the least hesitation or acceleration. His mind was a blank, but he approached the man as if he knew exactly what he was going to do. For his part, Israel didn't recognize him, but was uncomfortably aware that something wasn't going quite right.

"Israel."

"Do I know you?"

These were the only words they exchanged. All of a sudden, María grabbed him by the neck, dragged him over towards a building, and shoved his head against the wall with all his strength. Israel was left dumbfounded. María grasped his neck with his two hands, staring him in the eyes. He had thrown his body weight well forwards, and was pushing out from where he had a foot planted firmly on the ground, to reinforce the pressure through his hands. He was so enraged that blood started to trickle from his nostrils. The blood wet his lips. He exhaled and Israel's face became spattered with tiny red splashes, some of them assuming the shape of a tear.

María looked left and right and experienced the strangeness of killing someone in the middle of the street, without anyone else being the wiser. Israel was offering no resistance at all, other than that naturally offered by a neck as broad and tough as his own: the most he could do was struggle to keep his eyes open; his pupils were rolling, floating in their orbs without focusing on anything…

María dragged him back a little way, and hammered his head into the wall once more. This time, the blow was far more violent than the previous one.

Israel closed his eyes. The weight of his body doubled at least. That was when María loosened the pressure in his hands.

After which he fled. He stopped only when he ran out of breath. He had the impression that everything had happened very rapidly and that he'd fled the scene of the crime so fast that Israel, now a mile or two behind him, was still breathing his last.

He sat down on a doorstep, in a block in the middle of a darkened street. A man came past, carrying a pizza in its cardboard box on the palm of one hand.

"D'you have the time?" asked María.

"No."

The man went on by.

María got to his feet, put one hand in his pocket and felt for the key to the villa. Then he sat himself down again.

A tramp approached, pushing a supermarket trolley loaded with cardboard he had collected and, without pausing on his journey, called out:

"D'you have the time?"

"No," replied María, and paused to wonder why a tramp would need to know the time. Probably the pizza delivery man was asking himself the same question about him. It had to be around eight – or possibly nine – o'clock at night.

The door before which he was seated opened unexpectedly, and a young woman almost tripped over him. She backed off in panic and shielded herself behind a skinny and pallid youth dressed all in black, with a woollen hat embellished with the slogan *PORN* in red pulled down over his eyebrows.

"Excuse me," the young guy said to him.

María stood up to make way for them.

The young couple made their exit one behind the other, and disappeared rapidly into the distance, arm in arm and whispering. María took note of where the girl had been looking: she had been staring at his nose. He touched it with a finger. Over his upper lip was a cascade, or a Hitler moustache, of dried blood. He tried to clean it off with saliva, but ended up having to wash it with water from the pavement gutter. He rubbed the cuff of his shirtsleeve across his mouth, drying it off, and walked over to the corner.

The next time he asked for the time, already in the neighbourhood of the villa, he was told it was three o'clock. Until that point, he had been walking without any sense of direction, while deliberately singling out the streets with the most traffic on them, on which he felt he could pass by without arousing the least suspicion – or less than on emptier side streets, with or without lighting. Ahead or behind, along the avenues, there were great pools of light drawing people in like moths around a flame: a cinema, a shopping mall, a discotheque, where people gathered like insects. Sometimes the point of convergence was wide, sometimes less so, but it was always surrounded by dusk or darkness.

On one occasion, if he wasn't mistaken, he had passed by that way arm in arm with Rosa, window-shopping and finding something to say about whatever they saw. Rosa enjoyed comparing the price of clothes with the cost of public services, or with food; she grew indignant as she drew up the list of those items she knew she could purchase in the supermarket and compared them with the price of a pair of jeans, or when she attempted to make the equation between that of a pair of tights and a dozen – or maybe even fifteen – trips on the bus (depending, obviously, on the value of the tights) or the cost of a month's supply of gas (whenever she found cheap tights, the cost of gas seemed to her to go up).

For a while he'd been walking along, fumbling with a piece of paper in his pocket. He took it out. It was a ten-peso note. The note must have been there since before any of all this began...

The first thing that occurred to him was to ring Rosa. For that he needed coins. A few yards further on there was a McDonald's. He entered, went up to one of the tills and took his place in the queue. When his turn came up, he asked for one of the set meals and to have his change in coins. Then he sat down at the one empty table, and devoured his hamburger with its microwaved chips without lifting his head, intimidated by the hustle and bustle, uncomfortable beneath the bright lights, paranoid at the difference between him and the dozens of young people coming and going from the adjacent cinema, and squeezed out by a large

171

family surging by with their trays, in search of a place to sit down.

He got up and left. In the doorway there was a public telephone. He dialled the number for the villa and in less than three rings he heard Rosa's voice:

"Hello?"

"Rosa, it's me. Whatever happened? You didn't turn up."

"María, I'm so sorry. I couldn't make it. I wanted to come – I was going to come – but the Señora had booked me a doctor's appointment and I couldn't refuse to go."

"Why was she taking you to the doctor?"

"Oh it was nothing… just a check-up…"

"Did you feel ill?"

"No, no, I had some kind of a bug and… what do I know about it? Lately, the Señora seems to be looking after me as if I were made of gold. So you went, did you?"

"Why wouldn't I go? I needed to speak to you. I was waiting for you."

"What about tomorrow?"

"I don't know if I can make it tomorrow… It was supposed to be today…"

"Where are you? I can hear a racket…"

"Out on the street."

"Ah, now I can make it out. Come to think of it, it has to be the first time there's been a background noise when you've rung me. Where were you calling from before, from a private house?"

"Yes…"

"I swear I'd reached the point where I was certain that…" Rosa began, before interrupting herself again.

"What had you come to believe?"

"Nothing. Nothing at all, don't listen to me…" said Rosa. She sounded disappointed, as if María's love for her would have been greater within the walls of a prison than out on the street.

"Listen, Rosa, I'm in a phone booth, and they're going to cut me off at any moment. Wait until I can put in another coin… Oh – but what did I do with all my change? Ah, here it is. Hello?"

"Yes."

"Hang on a second, I still can't find any change… Ah, here it is… What were you saying?"

"You were about to tell me something…"

"Oh yes. I…" There was a pause and then he said: "Have you grown cold towards me or is that my imagination? What's going on? Don't you love me any more?"

"Why on earth do you ask me that?"

"That's the way it feels."

"No… well, María… so much water has gone under the bridge since…"

"Didn't it make you happy to think of meeting me today, as we'd arranged?"

"Sure! I kept watching the clock every few minutes but…"

"Now, what time is it?"

"I can't come out now."

"I know. All the same, what time is it?"

"Ten past eleven."

"What did the doctor make of you?"

"Fine, all well. Oh, María!" Rosa suddenly exclaimed. "If for once and all you'd only tell me something real, like why you disappeared, why today we could have met up but tomorrow we can't… why you couldn't ever before! At the end of the day, all this is your fault!"

"What's all my fault?"

"You upped and left me… you never came back… left me to take the rap, and I paid it with my heart! There are times when I swear I hate you! Yes, I hate you, I swear it! And today when I was finally going to see you, I hated you more than ever, María. Will you forgive me all this one of these days?"

"You're asking me if I could forgive you?"

"Yes…"

"There's nothing for me to forgive you, Rosa! Today I wanted to see you precisely because I needed to tell you that the only thing I want is to be near you and care for you, and…"

There was a silence.

A bird flew overhead. María couldn't avoid following it with his eyes. The rarest of things: a white bird, at least five yards up in the skies over the Avenida Santa Fe, at eleven o'clock at night, flying in the same direction as the one-way traffic…

"Are you really never going to come back?" asked Rosa.

"One of these days…"

"I knew that was what you were going to say…"

"You need to understand…"

"I knew it…"

"What is it that I need to forgive you for, Rosa?"

At that instant the line went dead.

In the kitchen, inside the villa, with the telephone still in her hand, Rosa said:

"I'm pregnant…" knowing that María couldn't hear her.

"I forgive you," he said, his eyes filled with tears, and hung up.

28

Finally, here he was again, stopped outside the villa. A few blocks back he'd again asked for the time: three in the morning. The villa was in darkness. There was nobody out on the street. Very occasionally a car slipped by. That was when he saw a policeman heading towards him.

He felt a shiver run up his spine. He stuck his hands into his pockets, moved on, and doubled back on his tracks to take a turn around the block. Getting inside again was going to be far harder than getting out. How come he hadn't thought of this? As he walked past Israel's building, on his way back into the villa, he saw the lights illuminated on the fourth floor... The cop was no longer on the corner: he walked on up the street to kill his hunger and cold.

He felt an impulse to run for the corner and make use of the cop's absence to reach the door and get inside without being spotted: he controlled himself with difficulty. The key was already in his hand. There were about ten yards between the corner and the barred gate of the tradesman's entrance: he ran them looking over his shoulder, towards the street the cop was disappearing down, hands clasped behind his back.

He was on the point of putting the key into the lock when all of a sudden a man and a woman emerged from the shadows, with their arms around each other. They came along the road chatting, gazing at the ground, and didn't seem too startled when they bumped into him. María rapidly regained his posture and the pace of a normal walk he had adopted up until his brief delay beside the gate, and set off in the opposite direction to the couple.

He paused another fifteen yards further down the road. He was sweating. The man and the woman crossed the street... The policeman was about to reach the corner; another second and he would turn on his heel and start walking downhill towards María again. He got to the gate in the blink of an eye, inserted the key into the lock and turned it. He pushed at the gate, went inside, and shut it again. He completed the moves very slowly, muffling its creaking from the start, and eliminating them as he went through.

Then he hid himself behind the wall. Crouched there, he waited until the cop got to the corner and set off up the street once more, in order to feel safe in crossing the side garden and entering the villa at last by the kitchen door. That was the most dangerous part of it. The lights were out, but he couldn't be sure whether Señor or Señora Blinder – or Rosa – were just on the other side of the door, for whatever reason they might have (even in the dark) to be there: he had to avoid making the least sound, because the house trebled the intensity of any noise and someone could have overheard. At the same time he had to do everything as swiftly as possible: someone could pass by on the street at any moment and catch sight of him between the bars on the gate. Dozens of worrying risks occurred to him, but he managed to overcome them all, and reached the kitchen safe and sound. He leaned his back against the wall and stayed there a moment in silence, waiting for the beating of his heart to quieten, and for his sight to become accustomed to the darkness. Then he opened the fridge, drank a large swig of white wine, removed his shoes, and set off for his bedroom. It was a success story. All except for one tiny detail.

That afternoon the gardener had mowed the lawn and watered the garden plants. And María had covered one shoe in mud while he was crouching beside the wall, to avoid being seen by the police.

He only noticed all this the following morning. Alarmed, he ran downstairs and approached as near as he could to the kitchen.

Rosa was sitting there on a chair, looking pensive. In one hand she held the floor cloth and was staring at the muddy footprints over by the door. A moment earlier, on seeing the footprints, she had automatically picked up the floor cloth and was on the point of wiping clean the mud when something attracted her attention. It was this she was now thinking over.

She couldn't fathom who might have left those footprints behind, still less why they went from the door to the fridge, where, all of a sudden, they stopped.

29

Only a few hours earlier, Rosa was on her way down from the attic washroom with a heap of clothes over one arm. Her belly, which had grown substantially in the last couple of months, along with all the clothes she was carrying in her arms, prevented her from properly seeing the steps, so she was descending slowly and taking care. Suddenly the hand with which she had steadied herself on the banister moistened, and she unleashed a squeal as she stopped in her tracks. The clothes fell to the floor, Rosa grabbed her belly and screamed for Señora Blinder.

For an instant, María was on the point of going to her rescue himself. He restrained himself with great difficulty. Fifteen or twenty minutes later, Rosa and Señora Blinder flew out of the house at high speed.

Now María began pacing nervously, not the traditional "to and fro" pacing, but more like a constant "up and down"... In recent months, he had been closer than ever to Rosa; it was incredible he hadn't actually trodden on her heels. He phoned her every week. He had come across a book called *My First Child* in the library, which he had read from cover to cover, and he'd taken to giving her advice on what forms of exercise were still suitable, and what kind of diet she'd do best to adhere to. But it hadn't exactly been easy getting Rosa to admit that she was actually pregnant.

In the course of a number of phone calls, starting with the one in which he had invited her to meet up with him in the little hotel down on the Bajo, Rosa kept insisting that they meet up, until the matter simply dropped out of the conversation, as if she'd forgotten all about it. It didn't escape María's attention that Rosa had wanted to meet up while her belly was still flat and had dropped the subject – he even thought he saw in her a kind of fearfulness, now it was he proposing a new rendezvous, which she found difficult to know how to refuse – when her belly became obvious, something which seemed to occur from one month to the next. Eventually one afternoon a ruse occurred to María, as obvious as it was effective: he would tell her he had just seen her in the street by chance.

"When?"

"The day before yesterday."

"Tuesday? But on Tuesday I had to spend the whole day in the house."

"Well, then it was Monday. You were just coming out of..." María paused, hoping that Rosa would complete the sentence for him. But wherever it was he saw her was something that Rosa couldn't have cared less about at that point in time.

"And you didn't call me?"

"I thought about it, but no I didn't. You were with the Señora."

María knew that Rosa had been out with Señora Blinder.

"So…" Rosa said meaningfully, lowering her voice.

"Yes, I know."

They both allowed for an interval.

María was under the impression that Rosa had stopped breathing.

Then he asked her:

"Why didn't you tell me?"

"Because… María, I…" answered Rosa, and started to cry.

"Don't worry, everything will be fine," said María, to calm her down. "How many months are you?"

"Five months."

"And the father?"

"Oh my God…" said Rosa.

"Who is he?" persisted María.

It had been a while since María had known all about it, and he managed to sound serene, even in a way relieved.

"The Señores' son…" replied Rosa. "He raped me… one time…"

That came as a surprise to María. It had never occurred to him that the child could belong to Álvaro… Then, while Rosa told him the history (the harassment, the rape), he processed a million figures, at the end of which he realized that Rosa couldn't be saved: she was completely incapable of stopping herself from lying to him.

He further realized that to her it was easier to say (or to say to him) that the pregnancy was the consequence of a rape than of her relationship with Israel. But this was no longer a matter in which he had the slightest interest. In any case, to contradict her would be to reveal himself. All the same, he did his utmost to sound indignant:

"The bastard, I'll kill him!"

"He's dead," intercepted Rosa.

"I know, I know, you already told me... What a bastard!"

"There's no point in getting all worked up about it now... are you all worked up?"

"I swear to you, I'd kill the bastard."

"I'm asking you if you're angry with me?"

"How do I know? You've told me so many things all at once that..." he began. And he observed he wasn't at all angry, only anxious to elicit a response.

María noted a grain of gratitude in Rosa's reaction. He was as good as certain that Rosa was reproaching herself inside for having hidden her pregnancy from him all this long time. She might as well have confided in him (he heard, in her voice). The mystery of his disappearance would soon be transcended by the discovery of a new man, absent but generous, a man without a body, whose voice would caress her more than anything else could.

From that day onwards, María kept her company wherever she went. Not perhaps every moment of the day, but in a general way. Cooking, washing and ironing, watching television, whatever Rosa was doing, he would be close beside her. Every night, when he came and went in search of food, he went out of his way to be there outside her room, and watched her for a long while through the keyhole, monitoring her position as she slept, the rhythm of her breathing.

He acquired the habit of checking the expiry dates on tinned products for fear lest Rosa might consume something past its sell-by date, and helped himself to the least fresh fruits and vegetables in order to leave only the best for her. Each time a new issue of *Selections* arrived, he would use his ingenuity to smuggle it up to the attic for a while. He conspicuously left self-help books out for her edification, like *My First Child*, and any time he got the opportunity he would add to the shopping list drawn up by Señora Blinder items like yogurt or chocolates, meticulously copying her handwriting, in order to satisfy Rosa's possible cravings. Naturally enough, Rosa attributed all of these stupendous delicacies to Señora Blinder's kindness. María observed this through the change in the relationship between the women, as it became more like that of friends, or even of family members. In his role as an invisible spy, he never discovered the true cause of the change in Señora Blinder's attitude towards Rosa. But the result was spontaneous and, at times, very moving. All thanks in some part to him.

They left behind them the chats in which nothing mattered as much to Rosa as knowing why he had disappeared in the way that he did, or where he was and when he would return. It was good luck (for him, who hated evading her questions). Nonetheless, nothing stopped him going over things in his mind. And every time he did so, he came up against fragments (moments) in a love which he savoured in his triple role as husband, father and phantasm. In fact he had taken his relationship with Rosa to a stage where his physical presence had ceased to be what mattered: what obstacle was there now to his being her husband? And if he were the husband who loved her and Rosa loved him and was expecting a child, why should he refuse to be its father?

For example:

"I read the book you told me about, *Your Erroneous Zones*."

"Did you like it?"

"I gave up on it."

"Because?"

"Because it bored me. I read the first part... I don't know, it didn't seem to apply to me... The first bit is all about... Hang on a minute, I'll go and find it, it was lying around here somewhere... Wait for me, eh?" She returned a few seconds later.

"It says..." she began, and started reading aloud: "*Look over your shoulder. You will find you have a companion who accompanies you wherever you go.* I liked that bit. I remember reading it, and it made me think of you, I swear. Do you know what crossed my mind the other day? Look, this is what crossed my mind: that you were here inside this house. Believe me. The other day I found some footprints in the kitchen and I swear on my mother's life that I went around the house with a fine-tooth comb – to every point on the compass – at the end of which I felt so utterly empty..."

It was true. María had watched her go through every inch of the entire house, going in and out of one room after another, as if she'd suddenly gone mad.

"It goes on to say: *For lack of a better name, call your companion Your Very Own Death. You can choose to be afraid of this visitor or to make use of him. The choice is yours.* That's where I started losing the thread..."

They were chatting like an old married couple, like a workman and a maid, a married couple of the future transported to work on different planets – without resentment, without even questioning the fact – at a time when relationships within the working class simply "happened like that".

They never mentioned Israel. María was certain that Señora Blinder must have been aware of the fact that Israel had been killed, so it was safe to assume that she would have told Rosa everything (rubbing her hands while Rosa suffered the impact of such news, and wearing a wide if near-imperceptible smile), in the same way that she could have sworn that Rosa *knew* (but in too indistinct a manner to catch him out) that he had been the murderer.

They had reached the perfect pitch of mutual understanding. They were at this point when Rosa's hand squeaked and paused on the banister.

From this moment until the one when María came to know his son, nothing more or less than three years flashed by: that was the true duration of the three subsequent days for him. In fact, Rosa went in on a Tuesday and didn't return until the Friday, quite late at night. And the first thing they did (Señor Blinder was engaged on a telephone call, conducted while staring at the television) was to settle the baby down in Señora Blinder's bed.

"Are you serious?" asked María, when he next called Rosa. "It seems to me that this is something you need to change right now. The kid can't sleep in the Señora's bed, the kid needs to sleep with his mother, and that's you. Settle him down in your bed, so he can smell your own scent, and make sure you really *look* at him, do you hear what I'm saying?…"

The second matter was to find him a name. They left the bedroom, sat themselves down one beside the other on the sofa and (while Señor Blinder, who had just broken off communications, went off into the bedroom to give a compromising look at the little creature) they began reviewing the first names.

Anyone could see that Rosa was tired, and that the one thing she longed for was to go to sleep – if at all possible, beside her son – that she was making an exceptional effort to quell the Señora's anxieties, all the while she was attempting to resolve the queries around the sleeping arrangements. Should she also lie down in Señora Blinder's bed next to her son, or was the Señora waiting for her to tell her she needed to rest and spend a while alone with her son, in order for the two of them immediately to rise to their feet, to go and fetch him, and to bring him to his room?

While Rosa was mulling all this over, María learned which gender the baby was.

"What do you think of the name *Gonzalo*?" enquired Señora Blinder.

(A boy!)

"Oh no, Señora, pardon me for saying so, but," Rosa lied, "my cousin is called Gonzalo and I could tell you stories about him you wouldn't begin to want to hear…"

"Or what about *Federico*? *Federico* sounds very nice…"

"Do you know which name I like the best?" asked Rosa.

María bent his ear.

At that moment Señor Blinder left the bedroom with an air so resoundingly indifferent to Rosa's new son it was deafening. But María failed even to notice. All his attention was fixed on what Rosa would say next.

And Rosa said:

"José María. That was the name I'd thought of…"

184

Señora Blinder straightened her spine, arched her eyebrows, and let the hand which hitherto she had held extended towards Rosa's face – just as if she were about to intercept her – fall back to her knee again. Then, at last, she froze. It was but for an instant, but it was enough for María to choke with emotion.

"José María? Are you really thinking of that?" exclaimed Señora Blinder. "Doesn't it sound a bit... forgive me for putting it like this, but... a bit vulgar?"

"No, Señora."

"There are so many names far prettier than this one..."

"But it's the one I like..."

"José María..."

"That's what I was thinking of, yes..."

"What do I know about it?..."

"Don't you like it?"

"To tell the truth, not much."

"It's great!"

"Listen Rosa, you're the mother here. If that's the name you want, give it to him, but don't ask me to lie to you about it. It seems to me there are a million and a half other names more suitable than that one. I don't know... Think it over."

A boy! *A boy!*

And Rosa wanted to give him his own name! Good God, what joy, whatever Señora Blinder had to say about it!... Rosa was thinking of calling him José María! She had said so, and he had heard her. Her very words were: "I like the name José María!" All the rest of that list, the other million and a half names that remained outstanding for consideration... which one of those could possibly now usurp his own, what possible chance could they have?

"José María, Rosa, yes, José María, he has to be called José María, don't let them change your liking for it," he was telling himself a minute later, as the initial euphoria abated.

He had only just seen him the other day, in the most daring act he had ever committed since the day he himself was born. He had entered Rosa's room.

It was six o'clock in the morning. Last midnight, after breastfeeding him, and under the attentive gaze of Señora Blinder, Rosa had succeeded in taking the baby with her (against the musical backdrop of a tempestuous football match). Possibly she had gone to feed him still one more time. In any case, they were both now asleep in the same bed together. The crib (which Señora Blinder had rescued from some storeroom pile at the back of the house some days earlier, and which no doubt had been where Álvaro had vomited his earliest months away) was placed close at hand. Rosa hadn't even bothered to attempt to set him down there. She had taken him directly into bed with her.

He was magic, in every possible sense: he had a face, he had fingers, and he breathed. Up until that point, María had seen no more than a bundle, a little ball of pale-blue blanket fringes. Now, as he approached him, becoming slowly used to the darkness inside the bedroom, the profile of a head was revealed, the closed flower bud composed of cheeks, nose, chin and mouth, all bunched together in the middle of his face, as if his features were still being sucked back into the nothing from whence he came.

He came a little closer.

Rosa was lying on her side, her back glued to the wall, giving the baby practically all the space on the bed. She covered his feet with one of her hands… María leaned very slowly over him until his lips brushed his son's forehead at last.

Some days later, he would still be savouring the details of this momentous event (the emotion, the surrounding silence, the tenderness) to the visual accompaniment of Neil Armstrong stepping onto the ashen floor of the moon. He straightened up, turned around and left the room at such a speed his shadow remained behind him.

Rosa opened her eyes, suddenly uneasy. She cast her eyes about the room as if she felt it still contained another presence, and, at the end of the half-second's review, returned to her baby, who too had now opened his eyes.

She calmed down.

The baby didn't yet know how to smile, but he smiled and said *I am me* with his eyes.

30

"Rosa?"

"María, how lucky you rang…"

"What's up?"

"I had a horrible dream! I woke up thinking, 'I do hope he'll ring me and I can tell him all about it,' and here you are. I dreamed I'd taken José María out for his walk, around that square where the Lago de Palermo is, and…"

"Did you really call him José María after me?"

"And you told me never to ask again where you are? Every time we talk you ask me the same thing! Of course I called him after you. Why don't you believe me?"

"I don't know if I believe you. I just don't fall for it, and that's another matter…"

"Speaking of falling… Do you know where the planetarium is?"

"Yes."

"I dreamed I'd taken him down there to get a bit of sun, and all at once I saw you coming out of the planetarium. I was frozen to the spot, it was years since I'd last seen you… As I've told you before, you appear lots in my dreams, but in this dream I knew I hadn't seen you for ages and it froze me to the marrow to see you suddenly like that. You'd been to see some showing about the moon… And you had a beard!"

"Are you serious?"

"I swear it. And you had long hair too."

"…"

"OK, so then you grabbed José María and threw him up into the sky and then you caught him and… well it was OK up until that point… But then you started throwing him up higher and higher each time, and I got frantic, and in the end you threw him so high that it took the baby something like half an hour to come back down again! We were staring up at the sky, but he was nowhere at all to be seen…"

"A nightmare…"

"Horrible."

"Did he come down again?"

"Yes, he came back down and you caught him. But from when he went up to when he came down I nearly died. I was in such anguish, you can't believe it! I was all covered in sweat…"

"You know I'd never do anything like that."

"Yes, I do know…"

"Does he eat well?"

"He never stops!"

"And you? Are you looking after yourself properly, eating well?…"

"Yes, normally. Do you dream?"

"What?"

"Tell me whether you dream. I've realized that you tell me nothing, nothing about what you do… or what you dream… or…"

"I never dream."

"Never?"

"I sleep very lightly. That probably has something to do with it."

"They say it does you good to dream…"

"The dream about the planetarium ought really to have been my dream, since I don't get the bit about the name."

"…"

"…"

"How terrified it made me…"

"Was he scared when he came down again?"

"Not a bit. He was killing himself laughing!"

"You see?"

"…"

"…"

"Oh, María…"

"Yes, I know…"

"Could things ever work out differently… one day perhaps?"

"You look after the baby. That's your occupation. And it's the best way to ensure that things will work out differently one day…"

"…"

"I mean it seriously."

"The Señora buys him all the new products on the market for newborn babies…"

189

"What, to eat?"

"Yes."

"But don't give up on the breastfeeding, Rosa. A mother's milk is a basic necessity for a baby's good health. What products is she buying him?"

"Some little glass jars of puréed stuff. The paediatrician told me that he can now start taking a few solids, and the Señora..."

"Still keep up the breastfeeding, just the same. And don't stint on how much you give him..."

"Right."

"Talk to him while you're feeding, or switch on the radio..."

"You've no idea what a lovely character he has! Everything makes him laugh and then he makes me laugh too... Anything at all makes him laugh. Pull a little face at him and he laughs... The Señora gives him a kiss on the nose and he laughs..."

"Your saying that reminds me of something in *Your Erroneous Zones*, when they say: 'It is always worthwhile surrounding yourself with amusing people'..."

"Now he's sleeping like a dream..."

"You always keep him in sight, don't you?"

"I've got him here next to me... Shhh... wait a moment..."

"..."

"Yes, it's the Señora just arriving... We'll have to hang up..."

"Tell the baby about me, Rosa. Tell him about me."

"Yes, yes, I'll tell him, I'll talk to him... Call me later. A kiss."

"A kiss."

31

When José María celebrated his first birthday, María made his first outside call. He wanted to give something to his son.

He rang the house of his uncle in Capilla del Señor. It was a sunny Sunday and Señor and Señora Blinder had gone out together. He hadn't the faintest idea where they might have gone, those two recently hadn't so much as exchanged two words with each other. Rosa had gone out with José María at the crack of dawn, to have a roast-beef lunch, in the company of her friend Claudia. Claudia's boyfriend was the waiter in a rotisserie overlooking the River Plate, in the neighbourhood of Vicente López. It would make a good outing for the baby. So María made the most of having the house to himself to raise his voice precisely as much as required.

"Who is it?" asked the uncle.

"Me, José María. Listen carefully, as I don't have too much time… Is everything OK with you?"

"…"

"Do you know the bedside table in my room? Do me a favour: go and take a look, and see whether underneath it…"

"Hang on a second," said the uncle. "Which José María are you referring to?"

"Me, it's me, *I'm* José María! María! What other José María would I be referring to?"

"Where on earth have you been?"

"It's a long story…"

"Well, tell me something about it! Are you in the country?"

"No."

"That's what I thought. What happened? The cops turned up here three or four times, to see if they could find you. So how come you're managing to give me a call right now?"

"Is your phone tapped?"

"What do you mean?"

"The telephone. Has it been tapped?"

"How the hell do I know? Why on earth would my phone be tapped – because of you? No… what I'm talking about happened years ago, at least two or three years… Anyway, what do I know about it? They never returned since then. You know what a state this country's in now."

"Listen to me…"

"Are you all right?"

"Yes. Listen here, Uncle. Do you know the bedside table in my bedroom, the one on the right? If you're standing at the foot of the bed, on the right-hand side? Are you with me?"

"What were they looking for, drugs? They wouldn't tell me a sausage. Were you mixed up in that whole drugs thing?"

"No, Uncle, drugs had nothing at all to do with it."

"Well in any case, to me taking drugs is hardly a crime, eh! You can talk openly to me. Especially as now there's so much of it about everywhere." He lowered his voice, making it sound reedy, without meaning to. "Does what you were going to tell me about the bedside table have anything to do with dope?"

"Listen to me, you idiot," José María interrupted in exasperation. He spoke in a monotone, a low note that was pure resonance from his vocal cords. His uncle pulled himself up mid-flow. "Under the bedside table on the right-hand side you'll see there's a drawer. It's as thin as an eyelash. In it you'll find there's $250. In the drawer of the opposite bedside table, there's a little bell, half chewed-up and in the shape of a star. It's an old-fashioned baby's rattle. You are going to bring both those things and deliver them to a girl who works over here. Her name is Rosa. You'll find her here, you'll hand over those gifts on my behalf, and you'll tell her I sent them. Is that clear now?"

"Why are you talking to me in that strange tone of voice?" asked his uncle, after a pause.

"Because I know you," answered María. "And I want you to remember something: I'm watching you, both you and the girl. The police are out looking for me because I killed a guy, and believe me, that guy mattered more to me than you do. So if you don't hand over the rattle and the dollars to the girl tomorrow morning, I'll come after you, and when I find you, you'll finish up seeing only darkness for the rest of your days."

Then he gave him the address.

The next day, María's uncle rang on the doorbell at the villa. He had dressed in his best clothes (a checked shirt, an old-fashioned anorak, without a designer label and so dark it seemed almost worn out – in fact it was a mass of every sort of loose synthetic thread, and that was it – and a pair of cream Oxford trousers, which gave him away as gay). María could see him from one of the windows at the front of the house: the shameless old devil rang the bell at the front door.

Señora Blinder went to answer it. On seeing him, her first reaction was one of surprise. She would never under normal circumstances have exchanged so much as a monosyllable with someone like him, but under present circumstances, she found herself talking to him for a while.

Then she went back inside again. Rosa, seated on the living room sofa, was just finishing giving José María his feed.

Señora Blinder stood facing her, looked down at where she sat and, with a serious expression on her face, said to her:

"It's so strange. This has to be the first time in my life I've answered the door to someone who calls, and I learn the last thing I ever wanted to know."

And she held out a brown paper envelope to Rosa. Someone had written her name and address on its mauve surface in careful black calligraphy.

Rosa opened it. She took out the dollars and the rattle and sat there staring at them, open-mouthed. Señora Blinder told her that someone had delivered them on behalf of José María.

The slowness with which Rosa raised her eyes to look at Señora Blinder laid bare her deception and her guilt. But Señor Blinder was too absorbed in her own cause for astonishment to take note of Rosa's.

"I stopped and chatted a minute with this... 'señor' on the doorstep, and he told me his nephew is José María, that local builder you knew, the one who was said to have murdered the foreman... No doubt you'll remember the story better than I. He told me that he had sent this to you via him..."

"Yes, you're right, I do remember him now..."

Today was José María's first birthday, but he was still taking breast milk and hadn't yet started to walk. While his mother and Señora Blinder were talking, José María turned himself around and crawled across the living-room floor at top speed.

"Isn't it as if the earth had opened and swallowed him up?" Señora Blinder was asking.

"It's exactly like that…" replied Rosa.

"So how, then, did that *fellow* just turn up on the door-step to hand over these things, supposedly on *his* say-so?"

"I don't know, Señora…"

They were both so immersed in their own questions and anxieties that neither took any notice when José María set out to clamber up the staircase.

"Are you hiding something from me, Rosa?"

"No!"

"Are you in touch with this man?"

"No, Señora. I swear, I'd had no idea about any of this… It came out of the blue as far as I was concerned, too… It must be years since I've seen that guy!"

Señora Blinder stared at her for a second in silence.

"So, then, how come you gave the baby José María's name?"

"Because I like it… by chance. My father was also called José María. José María Verga. Don't make me repeat it – you know I don't like the surname…" went on Rosa, feigning embarrassment.

"And what was that workman's surname?"

"Negro."

"Negro?"

"Yes…"

"Do you realize," Señora Blinder added, having thought it over for a moment, "that if you'd gone on going out with him, you could have ended up being called Rosa Verga de Negro, Rosa Negro's dick."

There was another moment's silence. Rosa and Señora Blinder looked one another in the eye seriously, and then both simultaneously burst into loud guffaws. They laughed until their eyes ran with tears. The pair of them knew that it was about nothing, but on some level they accepted this way of releasing tension. As soon as it was over, they felt much better.

Señora Blinder came back round and seated herself down next to Rosa again.

"Why do you think that builder fellow would have sent you those things after such a long time?"

"I don't know, Señora... Who brought them here?"

"An uncle of his, apparently."

"And the uncle didn't say why?"

"He didn't know. Or else he didn't want to tell me. He said he'd heard nothing at all of or from his nephew for years now..."

"So then it's true!" said Rosa.

"What's true?" Señora Blinder looked at her enquiringly.

"That the earth opened and swallowed him up," said Rosa. "Nobody knows anything about him... I certainly don't..."

Señora Blinder believed her. There was no reason whatever not to.

"But it worries me that he should have sent you this..."

"Perhaps it means he's thinking of leaving the country..."

"I will have to keep the police informed..."

"They won't remember a thing about him."

"But that man could be dangerous..."

"Don't fall for that, Señora. He was purer than the Communion Host..."

Señora Blinder stared at her in silence. Rosa seemed to her either sad or exhausted, maybe both at the same time. She put an arm around her shoulders and said:

"You must promise me something... The very least clue you find regarding that workman, you have to tell me immediately."

Rosa nodded her agreement and, holding the dollars in one hand and the rattle in the other, kissed her fingers in the form of the crucifix.

32

That afternoon José María junior climbed twelve steps. María, poised at the top of the flight, counted them one by one in a mixture of panic and pride (pride in his proficiency and panic lest he fall). He gesticulated wildly at him, trying to scare him off, but the child only seemed to feel spurred on by this. At least until Rosa finally registered his absence. She shot up off the sofa at the speed of a rocket, spotted him, grabbed a toy car to tempt him and grabbed him from the top of the staircase, carting him back down under her arm.

As a rule, Rosa was far from careless with him. Although Señora Blinder (mysteriously, as far as María was concerned) helped her with the boy, Rosa continued in her role as maid: she was obliged to do all the housework with her son at her side, and it could happen that sometimes she was distracted or he escaped her. Joselito – as she was beginning to call him – was both restless and at the same time often lazy. He still wasn't walking even at fourteen months old.

He had the exact same face as Rosa…

María called her almost every day throughout the year. They talked about Joselito. Rosa recounted the amusing episodes surrounding him, and María told her to be careful around the sharp corners on the furniture, or with the plugs, and more than anything with the staircase, to which Joselito seemed to have become addicted. From time to time (and now only very occasionally from one time to the next) Rosa went back to questioning him as to where he was and when he'd be back.

Joselito said nothing (he didn't talk yet), but was obviously charmed by María. As María was with him every minute that Rosa was distracted (each time that Joselito was alone in his room, or in the living room, or in the kitchen – and more than ever when Rosa left him in the playroom on the second floor and set off down the corridor with her vacuum cleaner), María went over to him, picked him up in his arms, made faces at him, or gave him a toy he'd made out of balsa wood specially for him to play with and which Joselito immediately smashed to pieces, grinning from ear to ear.

He liked his smell, which lapped him like a flame, without either form or edges, the sound of his gurgles, his skin as soft as pollen… But nothing pleased him as much as the hiccuping laughs with which Joselito greeted his briefest of appearances.

He taught him to say "Joselito" ("Lita", he said), or "*auto*" instead of "*tutu*", and, as he could no longer give himself a name for fear that Joselito might go and repeat it afterwards, he also got the boy to call him "mama" too.

"Ma… ma," he said the first time, kneeling closely before him.

"Am…" responded Joselito.

"Ma…ma…"

"Am…am…"

"Very good! Now, let's do it again… Mama…"

"…ma…"

"You've got it! My goodness, what an intelligent little boy you are…" He congratulated him, all the while stroking his head, before starting over again:

"Ma... ma..."

"Ama..."

Rosa thought that Joselito was endowed with a vast imagination, because he was always going around looking for something behind doors or at the foot of the staircase.

"I don't know what's wrong with him," she told María on one occasion. "I'm right there beside him and he's going around the back of me, calling my name. He makes me really worried when he does that..."

"Worried? What about? He's just playing a game."

"No, he's not playing a game. I'm right there next to him, and he's looking for me all over... Kids of his age don't play games like that. It makes me scared he might have some mental problem..."

"No, Rosa, what kind of a mental problem would he be likely to have? Kids are just like that..."

"I'd so love you to know him... you'd be sure to get on so well with him!..."

It broke María's heart: the hour (or the age) had come for him to be seen no longer, not even by his son.

33

One afternoon Rosa was mopping one of the attic-room floors with a floor cloth when María suddenly heard her swearing. She erupted with a yell, a yell followed by a patter of feet across the floor. There was no doubt about it: she must have just seen the rat.

Rosa emerged from the attic room at high speed, running backwards. In a frenzy, she picked up the broom and went back in again. María could hear the noise of the broom handle being banged on the floor, here – there – all over the place, in an excess of violent disgust. The banging ceased a few moments later: Rosa re-emerged and ran downstairs. Had she killed it?

In all probability not, for she then came back upstairs with her packet of rat poison. She went into the room and, a few moments later, emerged again. She regarded the broom handle with grave apprehension: at the very least she had hit it.

"Revolting beast…" she muttered, and went off cursing between gritted teeth.

María waited until he was certain that Rosa wasn't going to reappear, and went into the attic room. The poison was distributed in little heaps, carefully placed in every corner. He collected it all up, piled it up on the bedside table, went down on all fours and looked under the bed and under the cupboard. The rat was underneath the cupboard as usual. It looked like a dark mass, immobile although trembling. It must have been terrified, perhaps even wounded.

He banged on the floor with the flat of his hand, but the rat didn't make a move.

"Come here…" he whispered, "let me take a look at you…"

He stretched out an arm in the intention of catching it, going so far as to stretch out his fingers in the shape of a spider, trying to get near to it… right up close until he touched it. At that instant he felt an icy burning in his hand. The rat had bitten him.

"Me?" he asked incredulously. "You've gone and bitten *me*?"

Between his index finger and thumb there hung a piece of flesh and skin. The wound, which had just started to bleed, was in the shape of a smile.

He collected up the poison, went to the bathroom, threw it into the toilet, before washing the wound with alcohol. As he left the bathroom, he saw the rat slithering down the corridor, weaving back and forth in confusion. It had no idea which way to go. María paused and waited for the rat to decide. Only when it finally did so did he start moving forwards again.

34

"How lucky that you rang, and just in time! We're just about to leave for the Mar del Plata!"

María was up to speed with the Blinders' intentions to leave the city behind (they were closing the windows and securing the doors), but he'd had no idea where they were off to. María had had no chance to ring her until a minute before they were due to depart, and it was more an act of daring than a lucky chance which caused him to do so then, for the Blinders were close at hand.

"Are you off?" he asked her in a low voice.

"Yes! At first I thought of staying put, but then…"

"You'll get to know the sea…"

"Yes."

"And Joselito?"

"Well, naturally he's coming with me."

"Buy him a bucket… teach him how to build sand-castles…"

"Yes."

"How very nice…"

"Neither the Señor nor the Señora are too keen on going. It seems as if they don't much like the Mar del Plata, but a married couple they know asked them along and they didn't really know how to refuse."

"How long are you off for?"

"I think it's for a week…"

"And they're going to leave the house empty?"

"Well, there'll be a watchman here, a policeman in fact. I overheard them hiring a guy…"

"And he'll be living in the house!?"

"Who?"

"The watchman…"

"Are you mad? He'll stay outside, of course! They've hired someone to be there day and night, outside on the pavement. Did I tell you that I've got the impression that their financial matters aren't all as smooth as they could be, if you catch my drift?…"

"Yes."

"Well then. It seems in fact they're going from bad to worse, so that…"

"And is Joselito doing well?"

"Divinely well."

"Does he still follow you around doing those odd things you told me he did, wanting to have you at his side, then looking for you all over the place?…"

"He hardly does that any more at all…"

A severe blow, this.

What else should he have anticipated? Children can forget anything at the speed of light… One week in the life of a child Joselito's age had to be like a decade in the life of a man of his age…

"Tell the Señora to buy him a bucket…"

"I'll buy him one myself!"

"Fine. Better still. And buy him a spade while you're about it. Do you know what's best to do? Build him a castle at the edge of the water, with a moat around it, and you'll see when the tide comes in that it'll wash into the moat and, if you make a door in the castle wall, the wave will come right inside and wash it away. You can even stick some twigs in the roof too, like flagpoles... But keep an eye on him all the time Rosa, so you don't lose sight of him – you know a beach is like an anthill and if you let him out of your sight you might not be able to find him again, eh?"

"Don't scare me..."

"No... OK. Or rather yes. Yes, I want to scare you. You can never be too cautious. It's the same with the water: waves look so pretty but beneath them there's always a current."

"You've no idea how much I'd like to be there with you..."

"One day we'll go there, all three of us."

Then, suddenly, María heard the voice of Señora Blinder somewhere behind Rosa, coming down the phone line:

"Come on Rosa, do please pick up those suitcases. Whoever are you still talking to?"

"With Claudia, Señora," replied Rosa, "we're just saying goodbye." And she turned her voice back to the phone to speak to him: "Fine, Claudia, give me a ring when you're back..."... "Oh I didn't mean that, what am I saying?" she hurriedly corrected herself. "I mean I'll give you a call. Fine, a goodbye kiss."

She hung up.

They left a half-hour later.

And they took ten days to return home, not a week.

María found himself alone in the villa for the first time ever. It was desperate, he missed Rosa and Joselito so much (he even managed to miss Señor and Señora Blinder!), but also because they'd left such a minimal quantity of provisions behind them. Not a single perishable foodstuff remained at all. In the larder there were tins of sardines and tuna, some jars of jam and sweet chestnuts, two bags of rice, three packets of beans, one box of crackers, some tea and herbal infusions and coffee, and little else. He found a heel of bread in a bag hanging on the wall, and under the table was a case of six bottles of wine. The fridge was unplugged and empty (other than a half-dozen eggs and a couple of stock cubes), its door left open. Anything he ate in the course of this week would be clearly obvious at the end of it.

But this was not the worst of his worries. From one of the first-floor windows he could observe the policeman standing on the street corner, his back to the villa. He was in uniform and without a moustache. María was not thinking of going out, not that he was now in any sort of a position to do so… The policeman was clearly working to a timetable: from eight in the evening until six in the morning. That only left María the option of leaving the house in broad daylight. Impossible.

The street lamps outside the house remained switched on around the clock, the same as the kitchen light. Other than that, the rest of the house was in darkness. María couldn't be certain he would remain unseen from the outside if he put on the living-room light – or one of the others in any of the other rooms – and so he made sure never to do so. But he fell into the habit of sitting in one of the library armchairs, or of settling down wherever else inside the house the light entered – to read or at least leaf through their box of files and papers, even watch television.

The first time he watched television he felt a degree of strangeness, because what they were talking about was exactly the same as years earlier, except that now he no longer recognized any of the personalities appearing on screen. And those who were still there years later, and who looked game to remain there for many more years, were phenomenally old, as if an incredible quantity of time had elapsed since the last time he saw them.

He slept for three or four nights in Rosa's room. He left off doing so when he began to smell his own odour in her pillow. On the first night he ran a fever, his body felt like an anthill, and he noted a degree of insensitivity in the hand bitten by the rat. He observed that certain of the muscles were painfully contracted: the involuntary contractions affected one muscle at a time, each one an individual fibrous filament, on one occasion in his biceps, on another in a thigh... In the morning he checked over the entire room. Rosa didn't store any secrets there (no letters addressed to her or written by her). In the bedside-table drawer he found the star-shaped rattle which he'd managed to deliver to her as a first-birthday present for Joselito. Above it and on one side hung a sketch in blue ink, possibly scrawled in Rosa's own hand, on the wall above the skirting.

He opened the wardrobe. How few clothes she possessed! Joselito may just have arrived in the world, but he owned more outfits than she did. Children's bodies grow at such a rapid rate; even so, children always seem to own more clothes than they can possibly wear. But as an adult, when a body has grown as much as it can, if you want to put it like this, then one is obliged pretty much always to go about in the same clothes.

This was hardly the case for Señor and Señora Blinder. Their wardrobes were well full to bursting. However, it was noteworthy that they too kept no secrets stored there, or at least – like Rosa – nothing written down on paper. Not one thing he uncovered during those first three or four days alone in the house was of the least interest in terms of disclosing secrets. Or else perhaps the Blinders kept them extremely well concealed or María was already fully informed about them. In the end it was disheartening: a lifetime, two long lifetimes which, up until now, had failed to produce more than a ghost could discover in the course of a few short years (a ghost able to employ no more than one sense, the sense of hearing, at that).

Nonetheless, he was able to corroborate or complete a number of details regarding the Blinders: Señor Blinder was a solicitor, suffered from high blood pressure, and was unhappy and obsessive. At some point in her life, Señora Blinder had set up an art gallery; she was a "social" alcoholic (there was not one single photo of her in which she didn't appear with someone at her side and a glass in her hand, despite the fact that in the villa she only drank at night and in bed); she used any number of face creams, adored pastel colours and in all probability maintained a secret lover, to judge from a variety of overly coquettish designer garments relegated to the back of the wardrobe. The most interesting thing he found in the Blinders' bedroom was simultaneously perturbing and disturbing: one of his little matchbox aeroplanes.

The miniature plane was in the top drawer of a chest facing the bed. No doubt little Joselito had abandoned it somewhere, and Señora Blinder had picked it up and deposited it there. Or perhaps Rosa had cleared it up off the floor, and assumed that it was a gift that either the Señor or Señora had brought him... Nobody said anything about the miniature plane: it was he who had learned of its existence there. Objects which *nobody* has brought to a given place, and yet *exist* there at least as a topic of conversation, carry a great potential within themselves by their very existence, even if they are generally relegated to the rubbish bin without anyone having given them the least attention. The world, the entire planet, is filled with things *which nobody has put in the right place.* He left the miniature aeroplane where it was and shut the drawer.

One night (he was now sleeping in the Blinders' bed) he was awoken by a strange noise. He got up hurriedly, bent on discovering the cause. It crossed his mind that a burglar must be trying to get into the house. He went over to the window and opened it a crack: the policeman was there, still standing with his back to the villa. Next he went down to the kitchen. He found an empty wine bottle had fallen over beside the dustbin lid, which had also tumbled over, upending it. That was what had caused the noise he'd heard. Rosa had forgotten to take out the rubbish... He studied the bin bag: it was tied at the top, but there were slashes in it, as if it had been clawed or bitten. Who had done this?

The rat.

He ran a hand through his hair and over his face, relieved, and went back to sleep.

He was hungry. The overlooked bin bag served him from then on as a source to raid for the remains of what little was left and which he had no further choice but to consume: a tin of tuna, another of sardines, three egg shells, a packet of rice, the wrappers of a couple of stock cubes... He opened the bin bag, threw out the remains, and closed the bag up again. On occasion, when he was particularly hungry, he'd try and cheat his stomach with a slug of brandy. Or he would prepare coffee or tea for himself. What he liked best of all was maté tea, but he could hardly drink a whole packet of the stuff if Rosa was not drinking it at the same time. So he took up the habit, after using a reasonable quantity out of the tea caddy, to dry the used leaves on the window sills.

He had begun having difficulty swallowing. He wondered if he might be suffering from angina, or the flu, but his throat didn't actually hurt him in the least: it was more like muscle spasms up and down his trachea, as if it were seized by an alien hand, holding him down by force and preventing him from swallowing normally, even from breathing at times. The fever came and went, rising and falling like a tide, and each time, when he retired, it left him with a different experience: unease, anxiety, more sensations of a crawling anthill…

He was irritable. One afternoon he broke the picture frame containing the portrait of Álvaro with a violent punch. He propped it down on the floor, knelt over it, and unleashed his full force behind his fist and against the glass. On another day he began running up and down stairs at full tilt, until he was exhausted. He had clenched his jaw so tightly in the process that his face ached.

At still other moments he was afraid. He had never been so alone in his entire life. Dr Dyer's description of a free man in the erroneous zones (combining an unusually high level of energy, a harnessing of the mind in creative diversions to overcome the paralysis that results from a dearth of interest) – in which he fully believed he saw himself described – fell apart without a sound. The silent footfalls of his bare feet wandering about the house aimlessly were in the end the only sounds he could hear.

When seven days had elapsed since Rosa and Joselito, together with the Blinders, had left the house, he took up a position near the garage, desperate to hear the sound of the car motor on its way home, bringing his family back to him. He was growing weak, he'd lost weight and his chest was burning. He slept on a carpet on the floor. His throat seemed to have closed over and he could scarcely swallow at all. His muscles were quivering here and there, all up and down his body, like nervous currents of light amid the serene darkness of the house.

One morning the dawn chorus of the birds on his window sill awoke him: they were squabbling. Then he observed that the noise of the traffic was considerably louder than that of the birds, and yet it seemed to him that it was the birds' squabbles he had first been aware of. Would he have heard the Blinders even if they had arrived? The disappointment at their non-appearance had intensified the burning sensation in his chest, and the blockage in his throat. He had spent a week on the ground floor; he needed to get back upstairs.

After a few hours in the attic he felt better, as if the time spent at ground level had harmed him in some way. That evening he went downstairs to make himself some soup. Then he decided to go back upstairs, but only as far as the third floor. He settled himself down in an armchair and began to drink his soup. His mind was a blank and his gaze was lost in space. At that moment the telephone rang. The soup plate slipped through his fingers and rebounded across the floor, spilling as it went.

It was the first time in a week someone had rung the phone. Most likely the few friends that the Blinders still retained knew that they were away from the house and would be back today. From then on the phone started ringing on a number of occasions: it was only the phone on the third floor, never the one in the kitchen, which rang. In all the time he had been in the house, he had never heard that phone ring once... When the answerphone cut in automatically, the person at the other end hung up. Could it have been Rosa? Was there any logic at all in imagining that Rosa was fantasizing about him being there in the house and was calling him from time to time, without the least expectation that he would actually pick up the phone, but by way of sending out a greeting?

He gathered up the fragments of the broken soup plate, plunged one hand into the rubbish bag, making a hole in it, and inserted them into the bottom of it... just in case. A nauseating stench emanated from the split bag. When he came to tie it up again, he saw that the scratches in it were now wider than ever: on one side of the bag there was now a split as broad as a handspan. His own hand and forearm, once inserted into the rubbish, smelled like something dead and decaying. It was a miracle to find them still attached to his body.

He took a bath, like one of those medical "immersion baths". At one point he submerged his head in the water and heard a dripping... *plick... plick... plick... plick...* He remained submerged until he had to come up for air. Then he noticed a little crack in the ceiling, from which thick drops of a dark and viscous liquid were falling in a rhythm which grew to a crescendo as they crashed into the water. On contact, the drops spread out, staining the water red. Blood. Was he hallucinating? He squeezed his eyes tight shut and when he reopened them, the crack was still there. But now it had increased in size and the blood was dripping from various different points at the same time... He stared fixedly at it, until the crack disappeared and the water appeared clear once more. When he decided to get back out of the bath, he realized he had lost all his agility: he had the sensation of having aged fifty years in fifty minutes. He got to his feet, dried and dressed himself, but each of these actions demanded the strength of Hercules.

Then, all of a sudden and at last, a half-hour later, it was as if absolutely nothing had occurred.

He was utterly exhausted and running a high temperature. He crawled in the direction of light and air, then sat down on the floor, one arm extended towards the window. He closed his eyes and fell asleep. The telephone resumed its ringing... When it stopped, he was under the impression that some idea or other had escaped from his head, or perhaps it was a memory, or a thought, he couldn't be sure. But he somehow reached the conclusion that this was something which was occurring with increasing frequency: little jumps or connections inside his mind departing one after another endlessly. He spent a long while trying to follow the shape these thoughts were assuming, as if they rose and fell, isolated and disconnected. An initial thought was continually unable to access the next or relate to it: he thought in bubbles.

Something caused him to open his eyes. It was already night now, but it wasn't really night-time. There were seven, eight, maybe ten rats on the staircase, some of them clinging to the wall, others being a little more adventurous in coming forwards... He wanted to get up but was incapable of moving: his body was as heavy as if he were still asleep. He slid along the floor. The rats scarcely budged. Only when he banged with the palm of his hand did they vanish as if by magic. Finally he succeeded in getting to his feet. He went to his room, entered it, and locked the door from the inside, stretched himself out on the bed and, despite the tightening in his throat and a body riddled with cramps, he went back to sleep again.

35

"Rosa…"

"María, my love!"

"How lovely that…"

"I've missed you!"

"…you're telling me…" María's voice sounded feeble.

"You've no idea what a good time we had… the best you could possibly imagine!…"

"And Joselito?"

"He went crazy! He was scurrying here and there like a wind-up toy, there was no way of stopping him at all! Just the same, we didn't get to the beach all that often. We must have gone there four or five times, one day on and the next off, because I stayed back at the house with those people, helping out Estela, a really fantastic young girl who works there for them. We became great friends, and I'll tell you all about it later… But Joselito, yes, Joselito went to the beach every single day. When I didn't take him there, he went with the Señora. You can't imagine how brown he now is!"

"Did you build the castle with him?…"

"I built thousands with him!"

"And with the…" – here he had to swallow hard – "the moat?"

"That as well. But he spent most of the time playing ball. What a great way of getting him to amuse himself! I swear that just to see him… You were so right, I was bound to love it there."

"You see?…"

"Why are you talking like that?"

"What do you mean, 'like that'?"

"Like that. Is something wrong with you?"

"No… I've got a bit of a sore throat…"

"Did you get someone to look at it?"

"No, it's nothing, it'll soon get better… Go on, tell me more about it…"

"I thought about you every single day. I thought how great it would be if I'd known the phone number there in advance, so that you could have called me… or if I knew your number… I talked a lot with that girl Estela… All the time, really, I so wanted to talk about you and… You've no idea how horrible it is not to be able to say anything to anyone, because on top of it all… well, as I told you just now, I missed you so much, oh I don't know… maybe it was because we'd talked of going to Mar del Plata, the two of us together, so often…"

"We'll get to go there…"

"…and they had an amazing seaside villa there, in a wood too, you've no idea how pretty it was. And the town centre, oh my God! I've never seen a town centre like that before. It's just like you told me it would be: a real anthill. On the beach or in the town centre, wherever you set foot, there were a million other feet next to yours. María?"

"Yes?"

"I brought you something back."

"What?…"

"A present. I've brought you back a present."

"Thank you, Rosa…"

"Two presents, in fact."

"There was no need…"

"I brought you a box of chocolate *alfajores,* made by Havanna, the best brand. Also a lovely necklace, with lots of little coloured stones. I know there's no way of telling when I can give it to you, but all the same it shows I was thinking of you and... Well" – she laughed a little – "if I end up eating the *alfajores* with Joselito, I'll still hang onto the necklace for as long as it takes. You're going to like it, just wait and see..."

"Thank you."

"I remember how you told me one day you liked the way necklaces could look on a man, that time we saw those guys wearing the beads... What a bad cough you have, María! Are you smoking heavily at the moment?"

"I don't smoke..."

"Have you given up?"

"I did some time ago... But tell me about Joselito... Did he sleep beside you?"

"All the time. The only problem is that he doesn't want to speak. He's hopeless! The one word he keeps saying is 'mama'. He uses it with me and with any man he meets – he doesn't call other women anything. And what about you? Tell me something about yourself now..."

"Nothing..."

"Haven't you got anything at all to tell me?"

"I love you, Rosa..."

"Did you miss me?"

"I missed you and I love you... both things are true..." he added. Just then he saw Señor Blinder coming up the stairs.

It was the work of a single instant: everything happened all at the same time. At precisely the moment María saw him, Señor Blinder called downstairs, without pausing on his upwards journey (and without giving him any time at all):

"Rita, come on, hurry up – please!"

María hung up at once.

He put down the phone and, with the last remaining shreds of energy, got himself up to the attic. His legs would hardly react any more… Going upstairs was like scaling a mountain… He went into his room, closed the door and sat down on the floor, his back pressed to the wall. He was sweating profusely and his hands were trembling. He was sure that Rosa had heard Señor Blinder perfectly clearly.

So he sat down on his bed and waited…

He felt weak and nauseous. It was very hot weather, that much he knew, but although he had put on his trousers and both his shirts, he was shivering with cold. In fact he could scarcely breathe… He had nothing more to give… He slowly turned his head and looked towards the window… He looked up at the light… heard the sounds of the street… He estimated it must be six or seven o'clock in the evening. Any moment now the darkness would begin to close in.

36

Rosa sported a deep tan. She had cut her hair back to her shoulders, and had put on some earrings with pale-blue stones in them, and which made her look younger and happy, although right now she was feeling dumbstruck. Her eyes were blacker and shinier than before and her nose had peeled a little with sunburn. Her eyelashes looked wet, as if they retained something of her last plunge into the sea.

Although more than a day had gone by since her return, she still hadn't resumed wearing her uniform.

She was wearing a one-piece outfit in the same colour as her earrings, and was as barefoot as he was.

It was nine o'clock in the morning. Rosa was standing stock-still beside the door. She had frozen into an expression of astonishment, both hands over her mouth. María had only to look at her to register that Rosa had been staring at him for a good while before he had managed to open his eyes. And she still couldn't believe her own.

María parted his parched lips to say something, but lacked the strength: so he closed them again, in a smile.

"Oh my God..." murmured Rosa, her hands still over her mouth.

Her hands were also deeply tanned, with the nails closely clipped and varnished, shining like mother-of-pearl. Around her neck was a necklace of tiny many-coloured stones. María realized this was the necklace she had told him about the day before, her present to him. Staring at one another like this was the first contact between the two of them, other than the sound of their voices, for years now. The recognition of her necklace was another, perhaps even more significant than the previous one, for it established a relationship between the two of them, over and beyond that of looking.

Rosa took a step forwards. Then she stopped again.

"María..." she said.

Another five paces further, one after the other, as if she were counting each one, until she reached his side. She held out a hand but, before she could touch him, she backed off again as far as the door, where she stopped. She was crying soundlessly. Joselito came into the room, running clumsily, then steadied himself by grasping the folds of his mother's skirts, as if he had just landed safely after jumping off a precipice.

Then he saw María, seeming more pleased than surprised.

"Mama!" he addressed him.

"*Hola...*" whispered María. So Joselito hadn't forgotten him.

Then, all of a sudden, Rosa ran over to the bed and embraced him.

"I knew... I knew!..." she said. "I knew... Oh my God, how long have you been here?"

"For ever..."

"And how come you never told me any of this?"

María smiled at her.

Rosa placed her hand on his forehead:

"You're raving!"

She looked wildly around her, towards Joselito – who had settled into tearing apart a best-seller – as if Joselito might be able to do something to assist her.

"In the room opposite..." commented María, gesturing towards the attic, "in my knapsack... take a look... I made so many little toys for him... some of them worked out all right too..."

Then Rosa came to and reacted. She got up, switching from a kind of stupor to highly strung nervousness, and began pacing from one side of the room to the other, considering what to do.

"Last night I finally realized all that was going on. It was when I was talking to you and I heard the Señor calling out for the Señora... but I couldn't bring myself to come up to the attic..." she shook her head. "Nighttime makes it easier to get out from here... I'll bring you something to eat, along with a glass of water, and I'll keep the door closed, and this evening we'll review how you're getting along and what we need to do to get out of here..."

Her ingenuity was touching. María was just finishing explaining to her that he had been there all along, and she was begging him to leave before another night should elapse. All in all, she was absolutely correct and rational: now she had discovered him, now he was no longer a phantasm, a suspicion, a possibility or a shadow, anyone else could just as well discover him too.

Rosa left the room. She closed the door, leaving Joselito on the inside, and set off downstairs at full speed.

Joselito was sitting on the floor, surrounded by torn and crumpled pages.

"Joselito..." María called out in a thin thread of a voice.

Joselito lifted his head and smiled broadly at him.

"Don't destroy that book any more..." María told him. "Come... come with me, Joselito... come here a minute with your dad..."

Joselito got up. It was hard work, but he got up. However, he remained rooted to the spot until María told him that he was going to tell him a secret.

Then he went over to him.

"Get up here, Joselito..." María said to him, patting his own chest by way of invitation. "Get up here and give me a hug..."

Joselito grabbed hold of María's shirt. María helped him clamber up, placing one hand under his behind and hauling him upwards, until Joselito fell on his belly onto his father's chest.

He hugged him.

It was an incredibly tender embrace, even though it demanded all his strength. Afterwards, while he invented a secret in order not to disappoint him, he shut his eyes and thought of Rosa.

218

He realized that he knew nothing at all about her. Did she have brothers and sisters? What was her first lover called? Were her parents still alive? He had no idea if she had a middle name... He was ignorant of the date of her birthday... He hadn't the least notion of what scared her, nor what she wanted from life... or from him. He had never asked what plans she had for the future... He wasn't even certain that she had plans...

Had he fallen in love with Rosa that day in the Disco supermarket? Or did that happen later, when he entered the villa... born of his secret, of the impossibility of being together with her?

Had he ever offered her anything at any time?

Did he know *who Rosa was*? No. In one sense, he had invented her. That wounded him. He felt the pain and decided that yes, in all likelihood he had invented her. But he would die with her son in his arms.

BACK TO THE COAST

Saskia Noort

Maria is a young singer with money problems, two children from failed relationships and a depressive ex-boyfriend. Faced with another pregnancy, she decides not to keep the baby, but after the abortion, threatening letters start to arrive. She flees from Amsterdam to her sister's house by the coast, a place redolent with memories of a childhood she does not want to revisit. But when the death threats follow her to her hiding place, Maria begins to fear not only for her life, but also for her sanity.

Saskia Noort is a bestselling author of literary thrillers. She has sold over a million copies of her first three novels.

PRAISE FOR SASKIA NOORT
AND *THE DINNER CLUB*

"A mystery writer of the heart as much as of the mind, a balance that marks her work with a flesh-and-blood humanity."
Andrew Pyper, author of *The Wildfire Season*

"Affairs, deceit, manipulation, tax dodges and murder – there's nothing Noort shies away from stirring into the mix, nicely showing off the sinister side of the suburbs." *Time Out*

"While there are echoes of Desperate Housewives here, this is closer to Mary Higgins Clark and is a good bet for her fans."
Library Journal Review

£8.99/$14.95/C$16.50
CRIME PAPERBACK ORIGINAL
ISBN 978-1-904738-37-4
www.bitterlemonpress.com